Eight armed men suddenly charged into the tavern.

The gunmen were dressed in gray overalls with large bandanna-style masks covering their faces from nose to chin. The shape of their eyes revealed that the invaders were Asians.

Voices cried out in alarm. Customers and hookers bolted for cover. The bartender ducked behind his counter. The gunmen ignored them and swung their submachine guns toward Mark Stone, Terrance Loughlin and Leo Gorman.

Gloved fingers squeezed triggers, and machine pistols roared...

D1007281

M.I.A. HUNTER
BLOOD STORM

JACK BUCHANAN

A JOVE BOOK

M.I.A. HUNTER: BLOOD STORM

A Jove Book/published by arrangement with
the author

PRINTING HISTORY
Jove edition/October 1986

All rights reserved.
Copyright © 1986 by Jack Buchanan
This book may not be reproduced in whole or in part,
by mimeograph or any other means, without permission.
For information address: The Berkley Publishing Group,
200 Madison Avenue, New York, N.Y. 10016.

ISBN: 0-515-08823-4

Jove Books are published by The Berkley Publishing Group,
200 Madison Avenue, New York, N.Y. 10016.
The words "A JOVE BOOK" and the "J" with sunburst
are trademarks belonging to Jove Publications, Inc.

PRINTED IN THE UNITED STATES OF AMERICA

"Go with us as we seek to defend the defense-less and to free the enslaved."

—from the "Special Forces Prayer"

Prologue

Sergeant Jackson collapsed in the ditch. At first, his fellow P.O.W.'s thought he'd fainted from exhaustion or sunstroke. But when the non-commissioned officer began thrashing about in a violent seizure, Lieutenant Nick Hall recognized the illness and jumped to Jackson's aid. He had seen advanced cases of malaria many times before.

A bamboo pole jabbed Hall in the ribs. He didn't have much meat to cushion the blow. Fat and muscle had nearly vanished due to malnutrition and frequent bouts of dysentery, diarrhea and malarial fevers. He had endured so much physical abuse he was almost immune to the jabs and blows of the guard's bamboo cudgel.

"*Seiq la-ah!*" Piggie demanded as he poked Hall with his stick.

The short, fat guard often spoke in his native language, which the American P.O.W.'s did not understand. "Piggie" was a Montagnard, from the Bru tribe. He had been a guard at the P.O.W.'s camp for more than a year. The Americans had never learned his name. They knew him only by the monicker they had given the fat sadist. That

1

was good enough. The son of a bitch looked like a hog that had learned to waddle on its hindlegs.

"Seiq la-ah!" Piggie repeated, jabbing Hall once more.

"What the fuck's his problem?" Corporal Dwayne Franklin muttered. A tall black man, Franklin was an ebony skeleton.

"I think he wants us to get out of the trench," Hall replied, rubbing his bruised ribs. "We'd better move Jackson fast."

The sun burned down on the men. It was a terrible, hot day to work, but every day for over a decade had been living hell. The P.O.W.'s were herded like cattle to the work sites. Hall wasn't certain what the project was for. It didn't matter anyway. Every work detail was pretty much the same. The guards stood watch. The prisoners hauled rocks, cut down underbrush or dug ditches to nowhere.

Hall felt as if he'd been a P.O.W. for a hundred years. His life before Vietnam seemed an ancient memory, an all but forgotten dream. He could barely remember what his parents looked like before he joined the Marine Corps in 1969. He didn't even know if they were still alive. The Communists claimed to have won the war. Apparently, they had—more or less. Maybe the Reds had taken over America as well. Maybe the U.S.A. no longer existed.

Hall didn't know what to believe. The only news which ever reached the P.O.W.'s was propaganda and rumors. Did it really matter if the United States had fallen? Either America didn't know about the M.I.A.'s who were still held captive or it didn't care.

Sometimes, he almost wondered if the United States had ever really existed in the first place. Maybe Colton Corner and the state of Indiana were only figments of his imagination, conjured up in his mind as an escape mechanism. Maybe there had never been anything for him except abuse, despair, and slavery in Southeast Asia.

The only reality Hall could be certain of were the Laotian soldiers and his fellow P.O.W.'s. Oppressors and oppressed. Masters and slaves, and a constant battle to survive from one day to the next.

"You American scum refuse to work?" Sergeant Phin demanded. The Laotian guard glared down at the P.O.W.'s, eyes narrowed into hard, dark slits. "Perhaps we have been too gentle with you shit-dogs. Would any of you like to wear the collar for a day or two?"

The collar was a device used for punishment at the camp. A large iron yoke was locked around the neck of the victim. Working with an additional fifteen pounds hanging from one's neck is a terrible strain for a man who already suffers from malnutrition and exhaustion. The collar was hollow, with a small opening which allowed sand or rocks to be added to its weight. The more serious the "offense," the greater the weight.

Occasionally, Captain Luang would order hot coals to be inserted into the collar. The iron yoke heated quickly and the victim's flesh would slowly peel and burn as red-hot metal pressed against neck, chest, and shoulders. A metal screen allowed oxygen to reach the coals and keep them burning. Hall and many other prisoners carried scars from this vicious torture device.

"Sergeant Jackson is sick," Hall told Phin. After twelve years in P.O.W. camps, he spoke Lao better than English. "He needs medical aid."

"Please, Sergeant Phin," Corporal Franklin added. "At least get him some quinine. *Xin aong lam on?*"

"You beg for help for this weakling?" Captain Luang suddenly appeared.

He approached the ditch. "Our medical supplies are limited. We can't afford to waste them on scum who are too weak to live."

The camp commandant was a small, wiry man with a hard face and black, almond eyes. A former member of the Pathet Lao, Captain Luang still had the mentality of a guerilla. His hatred of Americans had sharpened when a bomb strike destroyed his family's village. The bombs, he had been told, were American bombs.

"It amuses me to hear Americans ask for mercy," Luang sneered, a cruel smile curling his colorless lips. "What mercy did you show my people when you invaded our country and dropped napalm on our villages?"

"The man's sick!" Franklin declared. He stood to his full height of six feet and six inches of dark skin and bones. "You can't just let him die . . ."

"I can do what I please, you black baboon," Luang replied with contempt. "If you had a brain instead of the slave memory of an African savage, you wouldn't trouble yourself about what happens to a white American pig."

"Goddamn you . . ." Franklin hissed.

"Easy, soldier," Lieutenant Hall warned. "Remember where you are before you say anything else."

Franklin nodded, beaten before he began. They couldn't win against their Laotian captors. They had been in the P.O.W. camp for more than a decade. Long enough to have the bitter fact of defeat driven into them again and again.

"Get your slimy comrade out of that ditch," Luang ordered. "There is more work to be done."

The Laotian captain marched away. Phin and Piggie remained, bamboo poles ready for use. Hall and Franklin gathered up Jackson and hauled him out of the trench.

"Oh, God," Franklin whispered fervently. "Please, send him soon . . ."

"Knock it off, Dwayne," Hall growled. "It's bullshit and you know it."

"No harm in prayin', man," Franklin replied, as he climbed from the ditch and helped Jackson to his feet.

"You know what I mean," the lieutenant said, pulling one of Jackson's arms over his neck and shoulders.

Corporal Franklin had not been praying for the Second Coming. He was praying to God that the rumors were true. The South Vietnamese veterans claimed they'd heard stories from other prisoners, on other camps, about an American vet who was rescuing U.S. soldiers from tiger cages all over Southeast Asia. Supposedly, he whisked them out of the jungles to Thailand and eventually returned the guys to their homes and loved ones back in the States.

Bullshit, Hall thought. Franklin might as well ask God to send Santa Claus to rescue them and take them out of Laos in a sleigh drawn by eight flying reindeer.

"We can still hope," Franklin insisted. "You can't order me to stop hopin', Lieutenant."

"You pray if you want, Dwayne," Hall sighed. "It won't hurt anything, but don't start getting your hopes up. There isn't any M.I.A. hunter. Probably isn't any God either—at least not one that'll do us any good."

"Don't you believe in *anything*, Lieutenant?" Franklin asked, his voice a strained whisper.

"Yeah," Hall replied grimly. "Survival."

Chapter One

Stone felt someone touch his hip. Fingers moved lightly toward his pocket. He glanced over his shoulder and slammed an elbow into the guy's face. The pickpocket fell to the pavement, blood oozing from a split lip.

"Out of my sight," Stone ordered. He repeated the sermon in Thai to make certain the petty crook understood.

Like a frightened mouse, the pickpocket scurried into the crowd. Nobody paid much attention to the incident. Bangkok is the kind of place where people don't see anything or hear anything—unless there's a profit to be made.

"Bloke's just trying to get by, I suppose," Terrance Loughlin remarked with mock sympathy for the pickpocket.

"Yeah," Stone said dryly. "Aren't we all?"

Mark Stone was a big man, with the muscled reflexes of a hungry tiger. Officially, he was a private investigator with offices in Los Angeles. Unofficially, he was a man with a personal mission—getting fellow Americans out of P.O.W. camps in Vietnam and Laos. Stone had been a prisoner in one of those bamboo shitpits. He knew the horror and despair of a P.O.W. And as long as a single M.I.A.

remained imprisoned in Southeast Asia, Stone would keep going back to set them free.

So far, the former Green Beret had been fairly successful. Hired by friends or family of an M.I.A., he financed his missions at no profit whatsoever. He did it because it was an obligation, not an occupation.

"A bit annoying how much time we have to spend in these seedy waterfront dives," Loughlin remarked as he glanced at the gaudy, shabby buildings surrounding them. "You know, I've got my reputation to think of."

"It'll survive," Stone assured him. "After all, you've tarnished it a few times yourself."

"Just polished the wrong places from time to time," the Brit replied with a shrug. Loughlin was a former commando of the Special Air Service and, in Stone's opinion, one of the best.

"Here it is," Stone said, pointing at a flashing neon sign above the entrance of a sleazy tavern. "The Golden Butterfly."

"I had hoped we'd be able to avoid these drink-and-fuck mills while Hog was in the States," Loughlin sighed. "This place looks like the sort of a dump we usually have to drag him out of to take the big ox on a bloody mission."

"I just hope this Gorman guy is half as good as Hog," Stone commented. His voice implied he thought this very unlikely.

Hog Wiley was a huge, powerful asskicker from Texas; unpolished, uncouth, and rude. He was also one of the best fighting men Stone had ever met. Wiley and Loughlin were Stone's M.I.A.-hunting team, but Hog had been wounded during their last mission. The big man was stateside, recovering from his injuries. Hog had told Stone that he was "all healed up and ready to raise more hell than a whore at a Boy Scout camp", but Stone could not allow Hog to endanger himself or the success of the mission simply because the Texas hulk was overeager to get back into action.

Unfortunately, Stone could not wait for Hog to mend. He had been contacted by An Khom concerning informa-

tion about P.O.W.'s held at a camp in Laos. And since the
Communists shuffled prisoners from camp to camp to prevent enemy intelligence sources from getting a fix on their
locale, Stone had to take action quickly.

That meant he needed a replacement for Hog Wiley. He
contacted various people familiar with the international
mercenary outfits. Most of the top-drawer soldiers of fortune were already off fighting other people's wars, in
Africa, Central America, and the Middle East.

The only guy available with the necessary experience
and skills was a mercenary named Leo Gorman. Stone and
Loughlin were supposed to meet the guy at the Golden
Butterfly that night. Considering some of the rumors about
Gorman, Stone wasn't sure he wanted to meet this soldier
of fortune, let alone take him on a mission into Laos.

The Golden Butterfly tried to masquerade as a night-
club, but it was really just another seedy dump of a bar on
the waterfront. A plywood butterfly was mounted on the
roof. The gold paint was faded and chipped, and part of a
wing was missing. A couple of Thai streetwalkers tried to
lure Stone and Loughlin away from the tavern. A little guy
with a big smile waved some wrist watches at the pair and
began to deliver a sales pitch.

Stone and Loughlin ignored the distractions and entered
the tavern. The room was dark, illuminated by small colored lights of red and blue which looked like they'd been
ripped off a Christmas tree. Customers of at least four na-
tionalities sat at the tables and lined the bar. Many were
probably dope dealers, smugglers and assorted cutthroats.
Small groups of men clustered around segregated tables
and discussed business—probably illegal—in guarded
whispers. Hookers avoided these guys and concentrated on
trying to attract less formidable customers.

Smoke hung in the air like fog. Stone noticed the heavy
scent of hashish. A jukebox played a Billy Joel hit from the
late seventies. The tune sounded a little odd, sung in Thai.

Stone recognized Leo Gorman from a photograph. The
merc sat at a table with a bottle of beer in one hand and a

cigarette in the other. A young prostitute sat beside him. It's hard to judge the age of Thai hookers. Forty year old women look like they are under thirty. Teenagers look like they are in their mid-twenties. The girl with Gorman appeared to be about fifteen, which probably meant she was between eleven and fourteen. She wore an artificial smile as she chatted to the disinterested Gorman.

Gorman grinned at Stone and Loughlin as they approached the table. The merc's face was wide, with a large crooked nose and dark eyes that seemed to bulge from their sockets. His lips were thick and wet, as if he was about to slobber on his shirt. Gorman's dirty blond hair hadn't been washed or combed for at least a week.

"About time you guys showed up," Gorman greeted them.

"Say good-bye to the lady," Stone said in a hard voice.

"Get lost, bitch," Gorman growled, shoving the girl from her chair. She almost fell, but managed to keep her balance. "If I want anything from you, I'll whistle."

The girl opened her mouth, but decided not to say anything. She hurried away from the table. Stone and Loughlin reluctantly sat across from the merc.

"I understand you guys are lookin' for some local talent," Gorman commented as he gulped some beer.

"Maybe," Stone replied. "But we sure don't need anyone who attracts unnecessary attention in public. That crap with the girl wasn't exactly keeping a low profile, Gorman."

"In this dump, it's normal," Gorman said with a shrug.

"We could have met some place else," Loughlin told him.

"I like it here," Gorman smiled. "Besides, this is a good place to discuss business. Nobody gets involved in anything that doesn't concern him personally. You poke your nose into another man's business in here and you'll probably get a knife between your ribs."

"Okay," Stone began. "So you're not as careless as you look. I didn't hear you were careless, Gorman, but I heard some other things about you. Some sounded pretty good and some sounded like you ought to have a rope around your neck."

"Oh, yeah?" Gorman raised his bushy eyebrows. "Hey, you guys have names?"

"You won't need to know who we are if we decide not to hire you," Loughlin told him.

"Is this limey in charge?" the merc asked, directing the question at Stone. "I got the impression you were the boss."

"He'll be *your* boss if we take you on," Stone answered. "To be honest, you won't win any popularity contests."

Gorman shrugged. "You figure you'd win any, Stone?"

The ex-Green Beret stiffened.

"Don't be surprised," Gorman chuckled, puffing on his cigarette. He blew smoke in Loughlin's face. "You know a little about me? I know a little about you, too. Stories about you have been floatin' around for more than a year. A lot of people in the merc trade know who you are. Congratulations. I figured you would have gotten yourself killed by now."

"Some of us have a talent for survival," Stone commented. "You seem to have done pretty well at that yourself. I understand you were in 'Nam during the war."

"That's right," Gorman replied. "Killed a lot of gooks. Got medals to prove it too."

"I would have thought you'd have a collection of ears for a keepsake," Loughlin muttered with contempt.

"Nah," Gorman smiled. "But thanks for the idea. Maybe I'll start one."

"Not with us you won't," Stone said sharply. "Let's not waste time, Gorman. I know you're a mercenary. You were in Angola, Rhodesia, and probably Nicaragua. You've got plenty of experience in jungle combat. You already know who I am and what I do. It shouldn't be hard for you to figure out what sort of job I'm trying to put together."

"We going to 'Nam?" Gorman inquired.

"Laos," Stone corrected. "There's a P.O.W. camp about

forty kilometers from the border. They've got a number of Americans held prisoner there. Guys like you and me, but they weren't so lucky. They'll probably move them soon, so we don't have a lot of time to spare."

"Laos, huh?" Gorman puckered his lips as he considered the mission. "I'll do it for twenty-five grand."

"Twenty-five thousand dollars?" Loughlin glared at the merc. "That's bloody ridiculous!"

"Back in the states that's a year's salary for a fuckin' schoolteacher," Gorman replied. "But you don't need somebody to teach the gooks their ABCs. You need me. I don't risk my ass unless I get paid, fellas."

"Five grand," Stone announced. "Take it or leave it."

"Five?" Gorman shook his head. "I could make more money bustin' legs for loan sharks here in Bangkok."

"Maybe you could work for the drug traffickers in the Golden Triangle," Stone suggested. "That's one of the things I heard about you I didn't like, Gorman. Rumor is you used to be an enforcer for an opium warlord with a home base in Laos."

"That's a fuckin' lie," Gorman hissed.

"How do you suppose a rumor like that got started?" Loughlin inquired.

"Look," Gorman began, his voice hard with anger. "I had some connections with the Golden Triangle syndicates. Shit, if you're gonna do business in this part of the world, you need information. You need contacts who can get you across borders and smuggle in supplies and weapons. The opium network can do that and more. Sure, I've got sources who are part of that scene, but I was never a goddamn hired thug for any slant-eyed warlord in Laos or any other place."

"If the subject ever comes up again, we'll be certain to tell folks your side of the story," Stone assured him. "But we've got a mission to set up and since you're not interested in a lousy five grand . . ."

"Hey, I didn't say that," Gorman declared. "So I asked for twenty-five thousand. I didn't really expect to get it.

Don't you ever haggle over prices? I go down a little, you come up a little."

"I already told you," Stone insisted. "Take it or leave it."

"Five grand is a lot of money here in Thailand," the merc remarked. "I wasn't planning to leave the country for a while anyway. You've got a deal."

"I think we can handle the mission without this bloke," Loughlin told Stone. "You and I can coordinate the Laotians and go in without him."

"Laotians?" Gorman frowned. "You're workin' with gooks?"

"Laotian freedom fighters," Stone hissed. "And if I hear you call one of them a gook, I'll hit you so hard you'll be wearing your jawbone on the back of your head."

"Okay, okay," Gorman said, holding up his hands in mock defense. "I'll watch my language. No problem. Unless, you agree with his lordship that you're better off without me."

"We need another seasoned combat veteran," Stone admitted. He turned to Loughlin. "The Laotians have courage, determination and discipline. But, they don't have experience."

"All right," the Briton agreed. "Welcome aboard, mate."

"Thanks," Gorman grinned. "You won't regret your decision."

"We'll see," Loughlin replied sourly. He obviously doubted the merc's remark would prove accurate.

"Well, I'd better—" Gorman began.

He was interrupted by eight armed men who had suddenly charged into the Golden Butterfly. The gunmen were dressed in gray overalls with large bandanna-style masks covering their faces from nose to chin. The shape of their eyes revealed that the invaders were Asians.

Voices cried out in alarm. Customers and hookers bolted for cover. The bartender ducked behind his counter. The gunmen ignored them and swung their submachine guns toward Mark Stone, Terrance Loughlin and Leo Gorman.

Gloved fingers squeezed triggers, and machine pistols roared.

Chapter Two

Stone and his companions had reacted to the threat before the invaders opened fire, diving from their chairs to hit the floor, rolling away from the table. More than thirty rounds of 9mm Parabellums smashed into the table and chairs. Furniture exploded into kindling.

Stone rolled behind the jukebox and dragged his .44 Magnum from a shoulder holster. He had to wear an over-size jacket to conceal the big pistol while dressed in street clothes, but he figured it was worth the trouble. The monsterous mag fired a powerful 280 grain wad-cutter which could bring down anything short of a charging rhino. The sight of the big bore weapon was enough to convince most opponents it was a good time to retreat.

The eight masked men were packing plenty of impressive firepower of their own. Six gunmen were armed with French MAT-49 subguns and the other two held MAC-10 Ingram machine pistols. Lots of firepower.

Stone knelt by the jukebox and held the Magnum with both hands. He aimed around the corner. The front sight fell upon the chest of the nearest gunman. Stone squeezed the trigger.

The mighty .44 roared and the recoil carried the pistol toward the ceiling, raising Stone's arms in the process. The Magnum had claimed its target. The bullet nailed the enemy gunman right where Stone wanted to hit him—left of center, through the heart.

The powerful bullet ripped through the guy's chest as if it was made of cheap cardboard. The impact of the Magnum slug hurled the gunman four feet. He was dead before his body hit the floor.

Two gun wielding opponents swung their MAT-49s toward Stone's position and opened fire. Parabellum rounds smashed into the jukebox. Glass and metal burst from the machine, but Stone stayed put. He clenched his teeth and waited for the high velocity hailstorm to subside. There wasn't much else he could do, except try to run or stand up. Either way, he would be cut to pieces.

Loughlin and Gorman had also unsheathed their weapons and headed for shelter. The ex-SAS commando aimed his .45 auto around the corner of a pillar while Gorman pointed a 9mm double-action Walther P-5 autoloader at the enemy force. Both men opened fire.

Two masked gunmen cried out as bullets crashed into flesh. They tumbled backward. One guy managed to trigger the last few rounds from his French chattergun. He blasted chunks of plaster from the ceiling before he fell dead.

The five remaining gunmen scrambled for cover. One man dove for the end of the bar. The bartender responded with a cut-down 12 gauge shotgun he kept under the counter. A burst of buckshot splattered the invader's chest into crimson pulp and kicked his body against a wall. The gruesome mess that had been human slumped to the floor.

A three round burst from an enemy MAC-10 caught the bartender across the upper chest and throat. The man dropped his shotgun and fell behind the bar.

Stone aimed his .44 Mag and fired. The big lead wadcutter smashed into the forehead of the gunman with the Ingram subgun. The guy's skull burst apart.

Another gunman pointed his weapon at Stone's position. Gorman squeezed off three rapid shots with his Walther. A trio of bullet holes appeared in the man's chest as he collapsed backward and crashed lifeless to the floor.

"There's a back exit!" Gorman shouted. He waved his pistol toward the rear of the room. "Follow me!"

The merc bolted from cover, firing at the enemy gunmen as he ran. One opponent ducked behind the cover of an overturned table. Stone couldn't see the other man. He pumped a Magnum round into the center of the table top. The gunman behind the cover screamed and tumbled into view. The .44 slug had punched through the flimsy wood and smashed into the guy's right thigh.

A stream of full-auto rounds sliced air above Stone's head. Bullets plowed into the wall behind him. Plaster dust spat across his back. He still couldn't locate the last gunman.

Loughlin's pistol snarled twice. Enemy fire ceased abruptly. The Briton had either nailed the last opponent or forced the guy to retreat. Stone signaled to Loughlin to move out.

The Brit dashed to the back of the room. Stone followed, sliding backward to keep his weapon pointed toward the enemy's position. The room was silent. Most of them were dead. The guy with the wounded leg appeared to have fainted. Whatever happened to the last triggerman, he wasn't shooting at them—and that was good enough for Stone.

The pair found an open door which led to an alley. Gorman waited for them. The merc stood by the door of a dark green Volkswagen. He smiled at Stone and Loughlin.

"I always try to park my wheels where I can reach 'em in a hurry," Gorman explained. "Let's get the fuck outta here."

Stone and Loughlin did not bother to reply. The three men quickly climbed into the VW. Gorman started the engine and the car shot out of the alley. Two trash cans bounced off the speeding vehicle, splattering garbage into the streets as the VW swung past the Golden Butterfly.

"Any idea what that was about?" Gorman asked, steering the car around a fishmarket stand.

"I was hoping you could tell us," Stone replied as he reloaded his .44 Magnum.

"Nobody's got any reason to send that much firepower after me," the merc declared. "I don't have any enemies with that kind of clout. Leastwise, not in Bangkok. How about you, Stone?"

"A couple."

Suddenly, a truck pulled in front of the VW. The lorry blocked the street. A tarp flapped open at the back of the vehicle, and three Asians poked the barrels of RBS-001 rifles between the slats. Home-grown Thai weapons combining features of the American M-16 and the Soviet AK-47, the RBS-001 rifles were pointed straight at the VW.

"Shit!" Gorman exclaimed as he frantically turned the steering wheel. "Fuckers have backup!"

"I do think you're right," Loughlin commented, his voice calmer than he felt.

The car whirled in a wild spin as the enemy riflemen opened fire. Salvos of 5.56mm slugs pelted the car. Glass cracked. Loughlin ducked low in the back seat, an instant before the rear window exploded. Glass shards fell across the Briton's back and shoulders. A bullet narrowly missed Stone's left cheek, hissing past his face before it crashed into the dashboard. The car radio erupted in a burst of sparks.

Gorman tried to swing the car around to retreat, but the enemy had blocked that path as well. A yellow Toyota and a BSA motorcycle with sidecar formed a second barricade. Gunmen lined up behind the car with automatic weapons. The guy in the sidecar fired a MAC-10 machine pistol at the VW.

Stone and Gorman ducked as Parabellum slugs slammed into the windshield. It held for a moment, but the second volley shattered glass. Bullets smacked against metal.

Water spewed from the punctured radiator. Two tires were hit and began to deflate. Bullets pierced the backrest, inches above the huddled shapes of Stone and Gorman.

The mercenary steered the car as best he could from a crouched position and stamped the gas pedal to the floor. The Rabbit rocketed toward the Toyota. Gunmen ducked and brace themselves for the impact of the charging vehicle.

But Gorman swung the Rabbit toward the motorcycle. The guy on the BSA tried to swerve out of the way while his partner in the sidecar fired another volley of Ingram rounds. The VW slammed into them. The sidecar snapped off its stalk and hurled across the street. It tumbled violently, crushing the trigger-happy gunman in the process.

The motorcycle spun out of control, its driver desperately clinging to his bike as it plunged through the plate glass window of a small restaurant. Fortunately, the place wasn't open. There were no innocent bystanders hurt. The cyclist was thrown from his bike and slammed into a table. Man and furniture crashed into a wall and fell to the floor in a broken, bloodied heap.

The VW rolled around a corner and awkwardly careened toward the pier. More automatic rounds chased the fleeing Rabbit. Water and petrol poured from the car. Smoke billowed as a ruptured line spilled oil on the hot manifold. Two tires were flat and a third was losing air fast. The muffler and exhaust pipe dragged beneath the carriage.

It was incredible that the car still functioned at all, and a minor miracle that Stone, Loughlin, and Gorman had survived the ordeal without receiving any serious injuries. The enemy ceased fire, but nobody assumed this meant the battle was over.

Gorman kicked open the door as the car slammed to a halt. He reached under the seat and pulled an Uzi submachine gun from a hidden compartment. The merc shoved a magazine into the weapon and worked the bolt to chamber the first round.

"There's a grenade in the glove compartment and an assault rifle in the trunk," Gorman announced as he jumped from the car to the cover of the crates.

"But does it have a laser disc player?" Loughlin remarked, his attitude more sour than usual. Being shot at never improved his disposition.

The glove compartment was locked. Stone took a military pushbutton knife from his pocket. The four-inch steel blade snapped open. He jimmied the lock and the compartment lid fell open. Stone removed the grenade and a snub-nose revolver.

Then, sliding out of the car on the driver's side, he joined Gorman behind the crates. The enemy's Toyota roared onto the pier. Headlights flashed twin beams and soon found the disabled VW. Loughlin was about to get the FAL assault rifle from the trunk, but he had to abandon the effort when enemy gunfire erupted once more.

The Brit dove behind the crippled Volkswagon. Bullets raked the car, splitting the metal skin to burrow into the body of the vehicle. The Toyota bolted forward. Two gunmen leaned from open windows to fire their submachine guns at Loughlin's position.

Gorman thrust his Uzi around the corner of a crate and opened fire. A merciless burst of 9mm parabellums pounded the Toyota. Glass shattered from the window at the driver's side. So did the skull of the Asian behind the steering wheel. The dead man fell forward into the dashboard, his foot jammed on the gas pedal.

The Toyota leaped forward at an accelerated pace. One gunman leaped from a window and dove to the pier. Gorman hit the car with another blast of Uzi fury. Bullets chopped the other gunman to pieces as he hung from the open window. The Toyota raced to the lip of the pier and sailed off the edge. It nosedived into the murky water below.

The surviving enemy gunman slowly rose to one knee. His left arm hung useless and broken. The guy couldn't stand straight because his right ankle was shattered. Blood oozed from a gash in his scalp. But he still held a MAT-49 in his right fist and aimed the weapon at Gorman.

Loughlin's .45 Colt bellowed twice. The Briton pumped both slugs into the chest of the wounded gunman. The guy fell back against the plankwalk as he triggered his French blaster. A three-round burst shot into the night sky, a funeral dirge for the slain hitman.

Headlights announced the arrival of the enemy lorry. The big truck had not been able to maneuver its way through the street as quickly as the Toyota. It had found another path to the pier and approached from the east. Riflemen stood poised at the back of the vehicle, eager to gun down their elusive prey.

Stone glanced at the grenade in his fist. It was an M-26, standard U.S. military government issue, with an eight second fuse. He pulled the pin and held the grenade firmly, the spoon pressed down, then waited for the truck to get closer.

"Want me to get their attention?" Gorman offered, tilting his head toward the lorry.

"I'd appreciate that," Stone confirmed.

The truck kept coming. The riflemen held their fire, unable to locate a clear target. Gorman slithered to the side of a crate and opened up with a long burst of Uzi slugs. Bullets rattled against the grill and hood of the lorry. At least one 9mm round struck the windshield and punched a spider web pattern of cracks in the glass.

The riflemen swung their assault rifles toward Gorman's position. They did not see Stone lob the grenade until it was too late to stop him. The M-26 hit the plankwalk and rolled under the approaching truck. Crying out in alarm, the three riflemen leaped from the vehicle. They hit the pier and rolled several feet before the grenade exploded.

The blast blew the lorry apart. The cab burst into flames when the gas tank erupted. Metal seams parted and shards fell in all directions. The back of the truck flipped over the firey cab and crashed into kindling across the pier.

Stone broke cover and dashed toward the dazed riflemen. All three hitmen had been struck by flying shrapnel
when the truck exploded. One guy was busy trying to put
out flames which burned along his sleeve. Another was
attempting to pull a six inch shard of metal from his right
hip. The third lay on his belly, blood splurting from the
stump of his neck.

"Freeze!" Stone announced, pointing his .44 Magnum
at the two survivors.

He repeated the warning in Thai and Vietnamese, although the muzzle of a gun is an effective form of univer-
sal sign language. Both Asians nodded and raised their
hands in surrender.

"All right," Stone began. "Who sent you? Who are you
working for?"

He started to translate the questions into Thai and Vietnamese. Suddenly, a volley of full-auto fire smashed into
the captives. The pair fell and twitched violently from the
savage impact of the bullets. Then they ceased movement
forever.

Stone whirled, .44 held ready. Leo Gorman smiled at
him. The merc raised his Uzi and blew smoke from the
muzzle of his weapon.

"So much for those motherfuckers, huh?" Gorman remarked with a chuckle.

"I wanted them alive," Stone said in a hard voice.
"Couldn't you see they were unarmed and I was trying to
interrogate them?"

"Didn't notice that," the merc said with a shrug.
"Looked to me like one gook was reaching for a weapon.
You know, some of these creepy slants carry a knife or
small pistol in a pouch hidden at the back of the neck. I
might've saved your ass, Stone."

"Maybe," he replied. "But next time, don't be so damn
eager to start shooting men who've surrendered."

"You're the boss," Gorman said with a shrug.

Stone returned his Magnum to shoulder leather. The

mission had not even started and already heavy shit was coming down on them.

But from whom?

Stone had made a lot of enemies. The Communist governments of Vietnam and Laos would certainly like to see him dead. So would the C.I.A. and the I.S.A.

If Stone's success rescuing American P.O.W.'s from Southeast Asia became public knowledge, the American people would realize how badly the government had handled the M.I.A. issue. And as far as the U.S. government was concerned, Stone was a threat to national security. The C.I.A. and the I.S.A. had tried to stop him in the past. They had resorted to violence on several occasions, and Stone wouldn't have been surprised if the so-called intelligence community of his own country had ordered a hit squad to terminate him "with extreme prejudice."

Leo Gorman was another concern. The merc was good in a firefight. Stone couldn't accuse the guy of lacking courage or skill. Gorman had also been prepared for trouble. The extra firepower in his car proved that. So did the vehicle itself. The Volkswagen obviously had reinforced steel and shatter-resistant glass. Otherwise, it would have been torn to pieces during the firefight.

Did Gorman have a special reason to expect trouble, or was he just extra careful and a little paranoid? Stone didn't like the guy, but Gorman was a topflight fighter. And that's what he needed for the mission in Laos. But Stone still had his doubts. The hotheaded mercenary could be a great asset—or a serious liability.

Either way, Stone didn't have much of a choice.

Chapter Three

They managed to slip away from the scene of the gunbattle. Curious crowds gathered in the streets when they were certain the fighting was over. The police would arrive soon. The cops had a tendency to steer clear of the district and pretty much let the Thai version of Sodom and Gomorrah police itself, but this was too large an incident to ignore. The local residents wouldn't give any details about the firefight. They had too many illegal activities of their own to conceal.

Stone and Loughlin had left a Chevy sedan parked outside the waterfront district, and they found the vehicle where they had left it. Stone slid behind the wheel. Gorman joined him in the front seat while Loughlin climbed into the back.

Stone drove from the area at a steady pace, not too fast, not too slow. They had attracted enough attention for one night.

"Well," Loughlin began. "Our little covert meeting wasn't exactly a state secret was it? Guess you picked the wrong place for a meeting, Gorman."

"There's nothin' wrong with the Golden Butterfly," the mercenary replied, turning his head to glare at Loughlin. "You two should have been more careful about coming to the place. Somebody must have tailed you guys and called those gooks to attack us."

"Since you killed the two men who might have been able to answer our questions about who hired them to kill us," Loughlin stated. "I guess we won't ever know for sure, will we?"

"Are you tryin' to say something, limey?" Gorman inquired tensely. "Or are you just runnin' your mouth to make sure it still works?"

"Calm down," Stone ordered. He glanced from the road to his quarreling companions, trying to pay attention to both. "Haven't you two had enough for one night?"

"I just wish we knew for certain that this bloke isn't still working for goddamn dope dealers," Loughlin declared.

"Look, you limey shit," Gorman snapped. "I already told you that I never worked for any drug outfit in the Golden Triangle or anywhere else."

"And, of course, you wouldn't lie about such a thing, would you?" the Brit scoffed. "You'd tell us if you were a hired gun for an opium czar—or if you've had a falling out with the bastards and they want to get even with you."

"Keep it up," Gorman snarled. "You've just about convinced me to decorate the inside of this car with your brains."

Loughlin didn't say anything. He wasn't in the mood to waste any more words on the thick-headed merc.

"Where are we going, Stone?" Gorman patted a canvas duffle bag. It contained his Uzi and the disassembled FAL assault rifle.

"I'll drop you off at a hotel in the Kai Chi district," Stone replied. "We'll contact you in the morning and let you know when we'll be leaving."

"Fine, but I'll need a down payment for my services."

"Give the man some money," Stone told Loughlin, taking out his wallet and tossed it to Loughlin.

"How much?" the Brit asked.

"All of it."

Loughlin handed Gorman a wad of bills. The mercenary counted the money. Half of it was in American currency and the rest was in Thai *baht* notes.

"There's less than sixty bucks here."

"I don't carry large amounts of money," Stone explained. "That's enough to cover your expenses until tomorrow."

"Yeah," Gorman complained. "It'll have to do."

Stone parked the Chevy in front of a little hotel on Mongkut Street. Gorman headed for the building and Stone drove up the street. He turned at the next block and sighed.

"For what it's worth," he told Loughlin. "I don't like that son of a bitch either."

"I didn't think you did," the ex-S.A.S. man assured him. "I doubt if his own mother can stomach him."

"We don't have to like the guy," Stone stated. "He's a professional. He's good with a gun, handles a car like a stunt driver and he keeps his head in a firefight. We need a man like that for the mission."

"Can we really consider him an asset when we can't trust the bastard?" Loughlin asked. "You think that'll change when we get to Laos?"

"I think Gorman will do what's in his own best interest," Stone replied. "He wants money. That's probably all he cares about, but that's enough to buy him for this job."

"Providing he can't make a larger profit by selling us out."

"He won't get a chance to," Stone said. "When we get into Laos he'll have enough to worry about staying alive. Same as us. He'll fight the enemy because his own survival will depend on it. That's good enough."

"I think we might be buying a lot of trouble," the Brit remarked. "What if those gunmen were sent by Gorman's former employer? Or a rival gang?"

"We don't *know* that he ever worked for opium merchants."

"We don't know that he didn't, either," Loughlin insisted.

"It's more likely you and I were the targets of those hitmen tonight," Stone declared. "Or at least *I* was."

"You figure the Communists sent them?" Loughlin asked. "Or the C.I.A.?"

"Either one," Stone replied with a shrug. "The guys who tried to kill us were plain old goons, not professionals. If they had been pros, they wouldn't have charged into the Golden Butterfly and started shooting. They would have waited for us to come outside and nailed us on the street."

"I was thinking the same thing," Loughlin agreed. "The bar was dark and crowded. Difficult to find your target. Street would have been better. Fewer witnesses and no place for us to run for cover."

"They had enough men to cover that," Stone added. "For that matter, they could have hit us from both the front and back doors of the Golden Butterfly. Professionals would have tried to get us in a cross fire. Those guys were just cheap hoods who got careless and overconfident because somebody gave them a bunch of nifty automatic weapons. None of those clowns were very good with a gun and I don't think they had much experience with full-auto weapons. They probably would have done better with shotguns and pistols. Anybody with enough money to afford them could have hired that bunch."

"The Communists and the C.I.A. aren't the only blokes who could afford to hire a hit squad," Loughlin remarked. "Big time dope dealers could have sent them. I still say it's a hell of a coincidence those bastards just happened to hit us when we were meeting with Gorman. I don't trust that slimeball."

"Who would?" Stone said with a shrug. "That's why I dropped him off at the hotel instead of taking him with us to meet with An Khom. We won't give that joker any details about the mission, besides what he already knows, until we're ready to move. All we tell him is what he needs to know to do his job."

"I still wish we could have gotten someone else," the Briton muttered sourly.

"So do I," Stone admitted. "But we're stuck with Gorman. Try to keep a lid on your temper, pal. If Gorman does what we tell him and handles himself as well in the jungle as he did in the street tonight, that's good enough. If he does the job, that's all I give a damn about."

"You know, I haven't heard many details about this mission either," Loughlin complained. "When do I get to know more?"

"Same time I do," Stone answered. "Everything is coming through An Khom. I guess we'll find out more when we meet with him."

Half an hour later, Stone and Loughlin stood in An Khom's garden. The setting was peaceful, with cherry blossoms, jasmine shrubs and colored rocks formed in zen symbols. It was an emotional and spiritual oasis in a world which seemed to be filled with violence and treachery. An Khom gracefully led his guests to a teakwood table.

"Would you care for some tea?" the frail elderly Asian inquired, gesturing at the pot with a small, slender hand.

An Khom and his guests sat cross-legged at the table. The old man poured tea into small ornate blue and white china cups. His every movement had dignified grace. An Khom was a man who had accepted the price of advanced age and learned to be comfortable with himself.

Yet, this polite and gentle old man was also an international arms dealer. An Khom also took this in stride. All men are a paradox and he accepted his own. Stone had met An Khom when he first started hunting M.I.A.'s. They had become close friends since then.

The tough American and the wise Asian shared a sincere mutual respect, trust, and love. An Khom's insight and understanding of people and life itself was greater than any man Stone had ever known. They had come to regard each other as father and son. Stone valued this relationship very deeply, because he had never known his real father.

"I heard a a news report on the radio just before you arrived," An Khom began, thoughtfully glancing down at his tea cup. "There was a terrible gunbattle at the harbor tonight. At least fifteen people were killed."

"We know," Stone confirmed.

"I thought so," the old man nodded. "And this mercenary, Gorman, did he survive or perish?"

"Oh, he's still alive," Loughlin answered.

"You sound almost disappointed," An Khom noticed.

"I *almost* am," Loughlin shrugged.

The old man wrinkled his brow.

"Gorman is pretty obnoxious," Stone explained. "But he's a good fighter and he's about the best we can find in a hurry."

"You have doubts about this man," An Khom remarked. He was not asking a question.

"The jury's still out," Stone replied.

"Be careful," An Khom warned. "An enemy within your ranks is far more dangerous than one you can clearly recognize on the battlefield."

"I'll be careful," Stone assured him. "As careful as circumstances allow."

"And you must learn more about the circumstances of your mission," the old man stated. He raised his head as a man approached the table. "Good. Muang Tzu has arrived."

The stranger was almost six feet in height, unusually tall for a Laotian. A blue shirt and baggy trousers hung from his thin frame. He bowed in formal greeting.

"This is Muang Tzu," An Khom introduced the visitor. "He is the leader of a band of Laotian freedom fighters who have spent much time in the plateau region."

"*Suh-bye-di,*" Stone greeted in Lao. He bowed with respect to the fellow warrior. "*Chao suh-bye di bau?*"

"I am well, thank you," Muang Tzu replied in fluent English. "Would you rather converse in your own language or Lao?"

"There is no reason for me to mangle your language

when your English is far better than my Lao," Stone replied. "My name is Mark Stone, and this is Terrance Loughlin, my friend and comrade."

"Mister Loughlin," Muang Tzu bowed again. "Time is critical, as you know, so I shall get right to the point concerning the P.O.W. camp."

"Of course," Stone agreed.

Muang Tzu joined the others at the table. An Khom poured a cup of tea for the Laotian rebel leader. The old man was always a considerate host.

"As you know," Muang Tzu began. "my country has endured great turmoil. The Communists seized control more than ten years ago. We fight them as best we can. My group is a small band of peasants who have become soldiers to fight the enemy. There are many other bands like mine. The Laotian people still dream of true independence. Of freedom."

Stone nodded. He was patient with the Laotian although Muang Tzu had said he would get straight to the point of the P.O.W.'s, instead of repeating what Stone already knew about the Laotian freedom fighters. This was Muang Tzu's story and he could tell it as he pleased. Stone had been in the Orient long enough to realize few Asians come straight to the point in any conversation.

"We are not as well armed or experienced as the enemy," the Laotian continued. "but we know the hills and countryside better than they do. It is our land, despite their claims that it is now the property of the state. We attack them in hit-and-run style. That is the expression, yes?"

"That's right," Stone confirmed.

"Thank you," Muang Tzu replied. "But to attack opponents of greater numbers armed with superior weapons is not easy. We must study our opponents carefully to learn their weaknesses and strengths. We watch, wait, and eventually strike after we have learned enough to know what sort of attack has the best chance of success, the strength of the enemy defenses, and when they are most vulnerable."

"Reconnaissance," Loughlin commented.

"That is so," the Laotian confirmed. "While in the plateau area, we came upon a prison camp. It is located near the mountain ridge we call Xang Phou. The camp is quite large, with many guards and strict security. After studying the camp for sometime, we discovered the number of prisoners was remarkably small considering the guard force stationed there. There are only twelve prisoners, outnumbered by the guards more than two to one. The majority of these prisoners are Laotians or Vietnamese. However, three were Caucasians and one was a tall black man. I am sorry to say that during our last watch we counted only two Caucasians. The other man may already be dead. Of course, that still leaves the black man and the other two whites. We can not be certain, but we suspect they are American P.O.W.'s from the war."

"Most P.O.W.'s are from wars," Loughlin remarked dryly.

Stone gave the Briton a hard look. This was no time for Loughlin's snotty remarks.

"My band is small," Muang Tzu continued. "There are only six men in my group, including myself. Since there are about thirty Communist soldiers at the camp, we would be badly outnumbered. We considered joining forces with another rebel band, but I had heard much about you, Mister Stone. This seemed the sort of mission which would appeal to you."

"Indeed it does," Stone confirmed. "You say you only have six men in your group. What are you armed with?"

"Weapons confiscated from the enemy," Muang Tzu answered. "Kalashnikov rifles and some old Type 56 Chinese rifles. Very similar to the Soviet AK-47, but unfortunately not all parts are interchangable. One man has an M-16 rifle. The Communists confiscated many of these weapons from Americans killed in action and we confiscated a few from Communists we killed. Unfortunate fact is that the M-16 uses different caliber ammunition than our other rifles."

"Yeah," Stone nodded. "The AK's and Type 56 are 7.62 millimeter, but the M-16 fires 5.56 mill. How much ammo do you guys have?"

"Not much, I'm afraid," Muang Tzu sighed. "The only way we can get ammunition is to take it from the enemy, and that has been difficult to do lately."

"We'll supply some extra ammunition as well as grenades, medical supplies, rations, tools, and other equipment," Stone assured him. "We'll also bring some spare weapons, although your people will probably get to pick up some more guns from the enemy before this mission is over."

"Otherwise the enemy will be taking weapons off our corpses," Loughlin added. "Which won't make much difference to us then, I suppose."

"But I can not pay you for these things," Muang Tzu said, lowering his head with shame.

"I will supply the ammunition, weapons and supplies," An Khom declared. "I do not need nor ask for your money, Muang Tzu. I make enough profit from my regular customers. To know that tyranny will not be accepted, that men are still willing to fight for freedom, is payment enough. At my age, a man needs something to believe in. Men like you give this to me. I can believe that the best qualities of man will never be destroyed by dictators and Communist dogma."

"But doesn't Mister Stone require some payment?" Muang Tzu inquired. "I mean, he does this sort of thing for a living . . ."

"No, I don't," Stone answered. "I do it because I couldn't live with myself if I turned my back on those P.O.W.'s. You don't fight for money, do you?"

"But I fight for my country," Muang Tzu answered. "Laos is not your country, Mister Stone."

"But those men locked in tiger cages are my brothers, as surely as if they came from my mother's womb," Stone insisted. "You don't let your brothers rot in a bamboo prison when the only crime they committed was to accept duty in the armed forces instead of running to Canada. I'm not going to let that happen."

"And you, Mister Loughlin?" the Laotian inquired. "Why do you risk your life for men you do not know? For battles which do not involve you or your country?"

"Every so often I ask myself the same question," the Briton said with a shrug. "The only answer I ever get is 'what the hell, it's what I do'. 'Can't think of anything else I'd rather be doing, so this is it."

"Incredible," Muang Tzu whispered.

"I like to think so," Loughlin said with a shrug.

Chapter Four

A P.O.W. camp is living hell. This is especially true in Southeast Asia. In a part of the world where poverty and despair are commonplace, treatment of prisoners—especially American prisoners—is horrendous.

Mark Stone knew this from personal experience and he had raided enough bamboo black holes to know conditions for P.O.W.'s had not improved since he had been a prisoner in 'Nam. A P.O.W. diet usually consists of boiled grass, crushed into a sickly green mush which resembled pasty puke, some fish scrappings which the average cat would refuse, bamboo sprouts, and once in a great while, some rice. But starving men will eat things they never thought they could bring themselves to put in their mouths when they've learned the real meaning of hunger.

Starving men will eat cockroaches, ants, and earthworms. They'll pounce on rats, tear the rodents apart with their teeth, and devour the bloody raw meat. They'll pick through buffalo droppings in the hopes that some of the animal's food has not been fully digested before the beast shits it onto the ground.

Water given to P.O.W.'s is murky and foul, crawling

with bacteria. Dysentery is common. Stone had suffered it himself. He remembered feeling as if his intestines were burning up inside him. He recalled the terrible fevers, and the horror of pissing blood. Stone remembered how he tried to avoid having bowel movements because it felt as if his scorched guts were seeping out of him.

The tiger cages and man pits were filthy, filled with the stench of sweat, urine and excrement. Insects swarmed into the cells, infecting the prisoners with yellow fever, malaria and typhoid. P.O.W.'s seldom received decent medical aid. Most of the jungle camps barely had enough medical supplies to take care of the guards and commanders. Few would give quinine tablets or immunization shots to prisoners when they might need it for themselves.

Yet regardless of the wretched conditions, the guards hauled the men every day from their cells and forced them to work as long as a P.O.W. could still stand or crawl. The guards showed little pity for the victims. Stone remembered being flogged with bamboo sticks and kicked as he tried to crawl away from his tormentors. The sound of their cruel laughter returned in his nightmares. He would awake, covered with cold sweat, his body trembling.

Every second in a P.O.W. camp is agony. Every day is a lifetime of suffering, every night an ordeal of hopeless despair. Stone recalled staring through the bamboo bars at the moon, wondering if he would live to see the next day.

No man should have to endure such misery. No man should have his freedom, dignity, and humanity stripped from him—treated worse than a beast. The war was over. Vietnam and Laos had no legal right to hold American servicemen captive. That made the situation even more intolerable.

Stone thought about this as he gazed down at his teacup. Muang Tzu had told him more about the P.O.W. camp in the plateau region. The commandant was a former member of the Pathet Lao. That meant the conditions in the camp were probably even worse than usual. The American prisoners might already be dead, and with the monsoon season fast approaching, the Communists would soon move the camp unless they wanted to tread water for about two months straight.

"We have to leave as soon as possible," Stone announced. "Any reason why we can't leave for Laos first thing in the morning?"

"Why not tonight?" Loughlin inquired.

"We have to get weapons, equipment, medical supplies and the rest of our gear ready," Stone answered. "You and I can be ready in a matter of minutes, but we'll need extra gear for our Laotian friends."

"I anticipated that you would almost certainly accept this mission," An Khom remarked with a slight smile. "Arrangements for it are already in progress."

"As usual," Stone grinned. "You're one step ahead of me, An Khom."

"Only one step," the old man stated. "I did not prepare for extra weapons and ammunition for Muang Tzu's band. Let's see, you'll need 7.62 Russian cartridges. The regular NATO ammunition in that caliber won't function as well in an AK-47."

"You've been able to get it before," Loughlin remarked with a frown. He favored the AK-47 himself because it had more takedown power than the M-16 or CAR-15 which are 5.56mm weapons.

"Oh, I have access to about two thousand rounds," An Khom replied. "Will that do?"

"That would be most useful," Muang Tzu said, nodding his head eagerly.

"For a start," Stone commented. "Could you include two extra Kalashnikovs for the Laotians, and an extra CAR-15 for Gorman, with about four hundred rounds of 5.56 ammo?"

"We're really taking Gorman, huh?" Loughlin sighed.

"Afraid so," Stone replied.

"He's got an FAL and an Uzi," the Briton reminded Stone. "Why give him a CAR as well?"

"Because I want the calibers to be fairly consistent,"

Stone answered. "If he wants to bring his weapons along instead, that's his business, but he'll be out of luck if we have to swap magazines or he runs out of NATO 7.62 mill for his FAL."

"How are we going to get all this stuff across the border into Laos?" Loughlin inquired. "That's a hell of a lot to strap to our backs and sneak past the bloody border patrols."

"We'll figure that out later," Stone replied.

"Don't forget to tell me when you do," Loughlin muttered.

"I will," Stone assured him. "You help An Khom get all our gear together. I've got a little personal matter to take care of before we leave."

"You're not going to visit Coleman, are you?" the Briton asked, rolling his eyes toward the night sky. "Just let it lie for now."

"If Coleman and his Company cronies are responsible for the ambush at the Golden Butterfly, I've got to find out before we leave," Stone declared. "Otherwise, we might get attacked before we reach the Laos border."

"Who is this Coleman person?" Muang Tzu inquired.

"A creepy bloke who occasionally crawls out from under a rock to prove he can be a bloody pain the arse," Loughlin answered.

"Alan Coleman is a case officer for the Central Intelligence Agency," Stone explained. "He's been assigned to prevent me from interfering with national security. I'm a threat to my country's government. It's a long story and it wouldn't make any sense to you if I tried to explain it. Doesn't make much sense to me either."

"You don't know that Coleman sent those killers after us," Loughlin reminded him.

"I know Coleman and his agents have been trying to track me down ever since that C.I.A. bloodhound arrived in Thailand three months ago," Stone replied. "They've contacted half the underworld in Bangkok trying to get details about what I'm doing. Coleman has gotten a lot of information from other C.I.A. operatives who've been on my ass in the past and he's probably tapped into I.S.A. records and other government files on me as well."

"How did you learn this?" Muang Tzu asked, startled by Stone's statement.

"I've got my own intelligence sources," Stone answered. "Americans can't do anything in this country without drawing a lot of attention. Coleman stands out here like a sore thumb, running around with his pet goons, Donner and Lawson. Those three idiots might as well wear signs that they're C.I.A. spooks. Problem is, they're crude enough to figure the best way to deal with a problem is to 'terminate with extreme prejudice'. They're the type to hire a bunch of two-bit hoods to do their dirty work for them."

"Jumping to conclusions can be a very dangerous exercise," An Khom warned. "And you may well regret rash action, my friend."

"If the C.I.A. is trying to kill me, I'd better take care of them before the situation gets worse," Stone insisted, "especially if they've managed to keep tabs on me well enough to know where I'm going in Bangkok, who I'm with, and possibly where I'll be going on the next mission."

"I still think you should keep away from Coleman," Loughlin repeated, shaking his head with dismay.

"Yeah," Stone answered. "Well, I think he should stay away from me. The government doesn't want to do a damn thing about M.I.A.'s in Southeast Asia. They want to play it that way, that's their business. But, they'd better not interfere with our efforts to do something about it. You guys concentrate on getting our gear ready for the mission. Like I said before, Coleman is really only concerned with me. That makes this a personal matter."

"I just hope you're not going to stir up a bloody hornet's nest," Loughlin sighed.

"Before I forget—" Stone drew his .44 Magnum from shoulder leather and handed it butt-first to Loughlin. "Better get rid of this piece. I don't need any ballistic reports linking this gun with tonight's shootout at the Golden Butterfly. You'd better do something about that Colt."

"I can just replace the barrel and the extractor," the Briton said with a shrug.

"Might mention ballistics to Gorman too," Stone added.

"So I have to fetch the bastard?" the Briton growled.

"Try to get along with Gorman," Stone urged. "At least for now. Contact him at the hotel and then haul ass to Ubon. You know where the safe house is located there. That's the best holdout spot we've got close to the southeast border of Laos. I'll meet you guys there about oh-five-hundred hours, if everything goes okay."

"And if it doesn't?" Loughlin frowned.

"Then you're in charge," Stone replied. "Cancel the mission or go ahead with it. Whatever you decide."

"Take care," An Khom urged. "Remember the lesson of the wood carver. It is sometimes possible to cut away more wood, but it is almost impossible to replace wood after it has been cut away."

Stone nodded. He understood An Khom's warning. If he did not take action against Coleman, he might have another chance later, or the C.I.A. officer might draw back his horns for awhile. If he did take action, he would have to be careful not to make any careless mistakes, because what has been done can truly never be undone.

"I'll remember," Stone assured him. "Thank you, and I hope we shall all meet again in the near future, under more pleasant circumstances."

Stone headed for the garden exit. He stopped when a familiar figure appeared in his path. An Ling was beautiful enough to make any man stop in his tracks. Her face was lovely, with dark almond eyes, a full mouth, and class features. An Ling's lithe figure equaled the beauty of her face.

"Hello, Mark," she greeted with a sad smile. "Leaving so soon?"

"I'm afraid so, An Ling," the tough American replied. "I wish we had time to talk, but a lot of lives are at stake. I must go now, but I'll return for a purely social call as soon as possible."

"I have heard that before, Mark," An Ling sighed.

"This time I'll be back," Stone promised. He hoped he would be able to survive to keep his word.

"Oh, Mark," she sighed with disappointment.

An Ling was An Khom's teenage daughter. Since Stone regarded the old man as his friend, ally, and father figure, he considered An Ling as a sort of kid sister. However, An Ling did not share this attitude. She was infatuated with the bold American, and Stone found this a bit awkward.

"I must go, An Ling," Stone told her.

"I understand," she said.

Perhaps she did, Stone realized.

"Take care of your father—I'll be back."

"Take care of yourself, Mark."

She watched him depart. A familiar sense of dread crept over her. Every time Mark Stone left, An Ling feared it would be the last time she would ever see him. She knew he was a warrior. This was Stone's karma. He could not do otherwise.

And if he died on the battlefield, this too would be karma.

Chapter Five

Alan Coleman had a safehouse at the outskirts of Bangkok. The C.I.A. case officer was officially an executive vice president for an American corporation which sold exotic incense and Thai curios. His two principle agents, Keith Donner and Phil Lawson, were supposed to be his control manager and advertising executive. They had rented a small house and set up their "sales headquarters" in Thailand.

Stone doubted that these half-wits fooled anyone—except perhaps other C.I.A. operatives in Southeast Asia. Virtually everyone in the Bangkok underworld and intelligence reps from Thailand and other nations knew about Coleman and his pals. Hog Wiley referred to them as "The Three Stooges of Spying."

Stone hoped the trio of C.I.A. agents were as inept as Hog thought they were. He approached the safehouse, creeping silently among shadows, near the east wall. Stone examined the area with a Starlite scanner. The optic fibers of the nightscope increased weak light reflected against the surface of objects. The Starlite was better than infrared because unexpected glare did not temporarily blind the user.

He spotted a back cone mounted on a tree trunk. He recognized the device as a battery operated motion detector, cheap with a limited range and a high pitch siren. He couldn't pick out any electric eyes or surveillance cameras. There might be a sound amplifier inside the house, but this seemed unlikely. Anyone who put much faith in a thirty dollar motion detector, probably did not bother to invest much money in any high-tech security.

Stone reached inside his field jacket and drew a Beretta 93-R from a special shoulder holster rig. A silencer was already attached to the threaded barrel. He approached the tree, taking care to remain clear of the scanning pattern of the motion detector. He raised the Beretta and carefully aimed.

He squeezed the trigger. A three-round burst of 9mm Parabellum rounds smashed into the frame of the motion detector. Black plastic shattered. Wires and metal fell from the wrecked scanner. The special Sconics silencer had reduced the pistol shots to a dull rasping, but Stone ducked behind the tree in case the noise had been heard by someone inside the house.

He waited a moment. There were no sounds to suggest anyone had heard him. Stone moved to the wall. The east side of the house was dark. But somebody was home. Stone had seen shadows pass across the window shades on the west side of the small building.

Stone examined the framework of an unlit window. It was wood, not metal. Any alarm wiring not installed in the frame made it very unlikely the alarm would be activated by disturbing the glass. Vibrations carry better in metal than wood.

Stone took a roll of engineering tape from a pocket. He tore off several strips and stuck the tape against a pane of glass near the latch. Then he rammed a fist into the taped section. Glass cracked.

Stone rapped his knuckles against the tape once again and peeled the strips from the window. He peered into the room, a drab little kitchen with a card table and some folding chairs. Probing the inside of the window with his NATO button knife, Stone reached through the shards of glass and felt the edges of the frame with the blade. At last he found the wires.

Cutting them might activate the alarm, but Stone thought it unlikely. None of the safehouse security equipment he'd seen was very impressive, and this was probably a very basic alarm system. Stone cut the wires. Silence. He turned the latch, unlocked the window, and shoved it open.

Climbing over the window sill, Stone slipped into the kitchen. He drew the Beretta and crept across the unlit room to the doorway. Dim light and muffled voices reached out from another room at the end of a narrow hallway.

He approached slowly, pistol held ready. He froze when he spotted the two men.

Coleman was seated at a computer. A small, slender man, he was prematurely bald and wore a black toupee which resembled a shaggy skullcap. The C.I.A. case officer frowned as his fingers tapped across the keyboard and information appeared on the terminal screen.

"Shit," Coleman growled. "That's a goddamn two-o-one file. Who the hell cares about the bastard's personnel records while he was in the army?"

"Maybe they didn't know what you were looking for," Keith Donner remarked. A heavy set guy who looked like a former college athlete, Donner was living proof that the C.I.A. was hard up for men. "Why don't you try again, Chief?"

"This is the third time I've contacted those army jackoffs," Coleman replied. "And don't call me 'Chief'. Who the hell do you think you are? A fuckin' Indian talkin' to Sitting Bull?"

"Maybe he thinks he's Maxwell Smart," Stone announced as he stepped into the room and pointed his Beretta 93-R at the pair. "They've got a lot in common."

"Oh, Jesus!" Coleman exclaimed, jumping from his chair and quickly raising his hands overhead.

"Nope," Stone replied. "Guess again."

Donner glanced at a .357 Magnum in a shoulder holster rig which hung from the peg of a hat rack on the wall. Stone aimed his Beretta directly at Donner's stupid face.

"Don't even think about it," he warned. "Both of you, move over to the desk and keep your hands on top of your heads. Don't try anything cute. I'm not in a good mood and I tend to kill people real fast when I'm not in a good mood."

"Look, fella," Coleman began. "I don't know who you think we are, but you've made a mistake."

"Maybe you made the mistake, Coleman," Stone replied.

"How do you know my name?" the case officer asked.

"I know who you are and what you are," Stone assured him. "You and your buddy Donner are with the C.I.A. More evidence of misuse of the taxpayers' money."

"Look, whoever you are . . ." Coleman was still trying to play dumb. He was a natural for the role.

"That's Mark Stone," Donner declared. "Don't you recognize him from the photos?"

Donner was even better at playing dumb.

"Oh, fuck," Coleman groaned with dismay.

"Don't worry about it, Coleman," Stone told him as he walked backward to the hat rack and plucked the .357 from its holster. "I already knew you guys have been looking for me. We're all together now, so let's talk."

"Look, Stone," Coleman said in a loud voice. "There's no need to bust in here and threaten us with a gun. Why don't you put that thing down?"

Stone pressed the cylinder catch to the Magnum and opened the revolver. He dumped the cartridges out of the weapon and returned it to the shoulder holster.

"Why are you yelling, Coleman?" Stone asked suspiciously. "Where's Lawson?"

"He's not here," Coleman replied. "Phil had to make a trip to Hong Kong. Can't give you any details . . ."

"Tell him to come out here with his hands up," Stone ordered. "Or I'll kill you both."

"I tell you, he's not here," Coleman insisted.

"You've got to the count of five," Stone announced. "And: you'd better believe I'm serious, Coleman. One . . . two . . ."

"Son of a bitch," Coleman rasped through clenched teeth.

"Three," Stone continued the countdown. "Stupid reason to die, friend. Four . . ."

"Christ, Phil!" Coleman cried. "Get in here!"

The sound of heavy footfalls drew Stone's attention to a stairway extending from the office. The chunky figure of Phil Lawson charged down the steps with a lead-filled blackjack in his fist. He shouted an obscenity as he launched himself at Stone, who simply stepped aside. The C.I.A. guy crashed to the floor with an agonized groan.

Lawson's swan dive distracted Stone long enough for Donner to rush forward and grab for Stone's wrist. Donner moved faster than Stone expected. Powerful hands seized Stone's arm and twisted hard. The Beretta fell from his grasp.

Stone had underestimated Donner. That had been a mistake—a potentially lethal mistake. Swinging a left hook to Donner's thick skull, Stone rammed a knee between the beefy C.I.A. man's legs. Donner gasped and started to double up. Stone broke free of the big man's grasp and drove a heel-of-the-palm blow under Donner's jaw.

Keith Donner landed on his ass, dazed by the barrage of blows which would have put most men in dreamland. Lawson was starting to get up, but Stone saw the greatest threat was presented by scrawny little Alan Coleman. The case officer had move behind his desk and yanked open a drawer. Stone didn't think Coleman had suddenly decided to check on his life insurance policy—unless it fired lead projectiles.

Stone dashed to the desk as Donner prepared to seize a snubnose .38 revolver in the desk drawer. Stone's left hand slapped the top of the desk as he vaulted over the furniture and slammed into Coleman. He landed feet first, driving a powerful double kick into Coleman's narrow chest. The C.I.A. officer bounced into a wall and dropped his gun.

Stone grabbed the guy's shirtfront with one hand and thrust the other between Coleman's legs. He easily raised the C.I.A. man off the floor and threw him across the desktop. Coleman cried out when he hit the floor.

A flash of movement warned Stone of danger. He glimpsed the black leather shape rocketing toward his head in time to block it with a shoulder. The blackjack struck hard. Pain shot through Stone's left collar bone and his arm trembled in a muscle spasm. Phil Lawson snarled as he raised his lead-filled sap and prepared to strike again.

Stone punched him in the mouth with his right fist. Lawson staggered backward, but he still held the blackjack. The husky C.I.A. dude shook his head and charged.

He grabbed a metal trashcan and held it up as Lawson swung his sap. The blackjack smacked metal, denting the can on impact. Stone swung a snap-kick to Lawson's groin, and the C.I.A. agent howled with pain. Stone slapped the bottom of the wastepaper basket across the guy's jaw. Lawson dropped to the floor as Keith Donner lunged at Stone.

There is a common misconception that everybody in the C.I.A. and other intelligence agencies is an expert in judo and karate. This is actually the exception rather than the norm. Donner appeared to have learned most of his hand-to-hand combat on a football field. He charged with his head down, fists positioned at his ears.

Stone let him close in and abruptly slammed the waste-basket on his head. Metal folded around the guy's skull like a helmet. Keith Donner groaned and fell flat on his belly.

An unexpected blow between the shoulder blades pitched Stone forward. He lost his balance and started to fall. Instinctively, he caught the floor with his hands and glanced back at the man who had hit him. Alan Coleman was standing over him, preparing to kick the fallen warrior.

Stone's boot lashed back first. He braced himself on his hands and delivered a hard kick. Coleman gasped painfully when the heel of Stone's boot caught him in the gut. The case officer doubled up, coughing and choking. Stone shot up from the floor and whipped a backfist stroke across Coleman's face.

The C.I.A. case officer dropped to the floor once more, but Phil Lawson was back on his feet with his blackjack held high. Stone saw the sap move forward.

Stone dodged the blow. Lawson's arm whirled past him and Stone slashed a karate chop at the nape of Lawson's neck. The C.I.A. agent fell on all fours. Stone stomped on the guy's right hand. Lawson screamed as bones crunched in his fingers. He rolled over on his back, clutching his broken hand. Stone kicked the blackjack across the room.

Coleman propped himself up on an elbow and used the back of a hand to mop blood from his split lip. Donner moved slowly, moaning softly as he caressed his battered skull. Lawson lay on his back, whimpering and cursing about his crushed fingers.

"Had enough?" Stone asked Coleman. The Viet vet was breathing hard. His jaw was bruised and his left deltoid ached, but he still had plenty of fight in him.

Coleman shook his head. He did not try to get up, so Stone understood what he meant. Crossing the room, he retrieved his Beretta pistol.

"Now, let's get back to the conversation," Stone announced, pointing his weapon at the three C.I.A. operatives.

"What the fuck do you want?" Coleman muttered as he tried to climb to his feet. The case officer groaned and fell back on his butt. "Shit."

"You guys have been trying to find me," Stone began. "You've been all over Bangkok trying to get information so you can try to put me out of business, right?"

"So you figured you'd come to us first and kill us?" Coleman snorted. "Really bright, Stone. You start killing Company men and Uncle Sam will put a price on your head big enough to attract every greedy motherfucker who knows how to pull a trigger. You can kill us, Stone, but there'll be a dozen more to take my place and two dozen after that. You can't kill us all. And sooner or later somebody will get you, fella."

"I don't have much choice if you clowns have already decided to shoot me down like a mad dog," Stone declared. "How much did you have to pay those jerks to try to off me? Whatever it was, you paid too much. They missed, Coleman. All they managed to do was piss me off."

"What the hell are you talking about?" Coleman demanded.

"A gang of trigger-happy goons tried to blow me away tonight," Stone explained. "At least one innocent bystander was killed and it could have been a whole roomful of people from the way those bastards were spraying automatic fire—like they were watering a lawn. I suppose you guys don't worry about innocent lives. Just write them off the way the government wrote off the M.I.A.'s from 'Nam."

"Look, Stone," Coleman began, slowly rising to his feet. "I didn't hire anybody to kill you. If I had, I would have made sure they got you and *only you*. You're a fuckin' menace! A crazy whose brains got scrambled in Vietnam! I don't blame you. After being caged up in a P.O.W. camp it's no wonder you're batshit. But you're trying to fight a cause which doesn't exist anymore. The war is over, soldier boy."

"Not for me," Stone replied. "Not for the Americans who are still missing in action. Until they're all free or accounted for, one way or the other, I've still got a war to fight."

"Well, three cheers for the big man," Coleman sneered. "Maybe you don't realize that you're messing with American foreign policy. We're trying to establish friendly relations with the Socialist People's Republic of Vietnam. Not because we love the Commie bastards, but so we can compete with the fucking Russians in this part of the world. Thailand is still an ally of the U.S., and we want to keep it that way. The Company has been trying to keep a low profile here. We'll help the anti-Communist forces in Vietnam and Laos. But it's gotta be done slow and easy.'"

"Tell that to the three million Cambodians who've been slaughtered over the last six years," Stone growled. "Tell it to the American service men who are still held prisoner in Southeast Asia. Tell them how they can wait another ten years for you people to eventually get around to doing something to help them."

"You believe what you want, Stone."

"*Ohhh,*" Donner moaned as he sat up and shook his head. "What happened, Chief?"

"Shut up, shithead," Coleman snapped.

"Goddamn you, Stone!" Lawson snarled as he staggered to his feet. He still held his broken hand against his chest. "I'm gonna kill you for this!"

"You shut up too," Coleman ordered. "Are you crazy, Phil? You're threatening Stone when he has a gun on you. That's pretty fucking stupid, man."

"That's just keeping in character for you guys," Stone sighed. "I'm not sure if you're telling the truth or not, Coleman. If you did send those hoods to kill me, I want you to know they failed."

"I already told you," Coleman insisted. "I didn't send any damn hit squad. My orders are to ship your ass back to the States to stand trial. I'm not even sure what the charges are—and I don't give a shit. You belong behind bars, Stone. Or maybe in a padded cell at a loonie farm."

"Just back off, Coleman," Stone warned. "I was gentle with you jokers tonight. Next time I might not be so nice."

"Fucking bastard . . ." Lawson began.

"Shut up," Coleman ordered. "I'm getting tired of telling you that, Phil."

"I'm leaving now," Stone announced as he moved toward the door. "Do yourselves a favor and don't try to follow me."

He opened the door and darted outside. Lawson hurried to the desk and jogged behind it to search for the .38 which lay on the floor. Donner headed for the hat rack and drew the Magnum revolver from its holster.

"What are you two planning to do?" Coleman asked wearily.

"I'm gonna shoot that son of a bitch!" Lawson declared.

"Don't bother," Coleman told him. "And you stay put too, Phil. If any of us stick our heads outside this house, Stone'll blow us away."

"Not if we all leave the house from different directions," Lawson insisted.

"Don't be stupid," Coleman snapped. "If we tried to go after him now, he'd waste us for sure. You've studied the records on Stone. Face to face confrontation is his especially. The guy is an ex-Green Beret! We're not gonna take him out that way. Not just the three of us."

"Stone was just lucky. . ." Lawson began.

"He mopped up the floor with us, damn it," Coleman stated. "And he's probably even better with a gun than he is with his hands and feet. If we fight Stone on his terms, we're as good as dead."

"So we let him get away with this?" Lawson demanded.

"Yeah," Donner added. He felt he should say something and this was the only thing which came to mind.

"Stone isn't gonna get away with anything," Coleman assured his C.I.A. buddies. "We're gonna nail his ass to a goddamn cross. And I'm gonna tell you how we'll do it."

Chapter Six

Leo Gorman crushed a cigarette under his boot. Loughlin clucked his tongue with disgust as he watched the mercenary kick the mashed butt into a crack in the floor boards. The Brit did not like Gorman's behavior at the safehouse in Ubon. The place belonged to a middle-aged couple who had fled Vietnam when Saigon fell. The Nguyens allowed Mark Stone and his allies to use their home as a safehouse during missions.

"You ought to show a bit of respect for other people's property," Loughlin told the mercenary.

"Hey, I'm a veteran of the goddamn Vietnam war, remember?" Gorman replied gruffly. "I risked my ass for those fish-faced fucks. They owe me."

"I do believe you are the most obnoxious bastard I've ever met in my life," Loughlin declared. His eyes narrowed with anger and his fingers flexed into fists.

"Well, that just breaks my heart," Gorman said with a smile. "So you don't like me. Big deal. You man enough to do anything about it?"

"Now that would be a pleasure," the Briton replied.

"Please," Muang Tzu said. The Laotian freedom fighter

had sensed the animosity between Loughlin and Gorman. He did not want to get involved, but he did not want them to kill each other either. "We should save the fighting for the Communists . . ."

"Butt out, slant-eyes," Gorman snapped. "This is none of your business."

"I believe this mission is my business, Mister Gorman," Muang Tzu declared.

"You want to mess with me too, gook?" Gorman snickered. He glared at Loughlin. "Looks like I'll have to take you both on at the same time."

"No way, Gorman," the Briton replied. "I want you all to myself."

"Xin aong lam on," Mister Nguyen whispered urgently. *"Thua khang day nay!"*

"Co tyu," Loughlin said with a nod.

"What are you two yapping about?" Gorman demanded.

"Mister Nguyen doesn't want us to fight in his house," Loughlin explained. "I assured him we wouldn't."

"No guts, huh?" Gorman sneered.

"I don't want to splash your blood all over Mister Nguyen's home," the Briton answered.

Muang Tzu frowned as he watched the pair quarrel. Loughlin and Gorman were both dressed in camouflage fatigues. They were armed with pistols, combat knives and a few handgrenades. Gorman also carried an Uzi which hung from a shoulder strap. Either man could kill the other in the blink of an eye. Perhaps they would both be killed.

He could not allow that to happen. The success of their mission depended on it. They couldn't afford to lose either Loughlin or Gorman. Muang Tzu had to stop them before the heated argument led to violence.

"This talk of bloodshed must cease," the Laotian declared. He drew a Government Issue 1911A1 Colt from a hip holster and aimed it in the general direction of Loughlin and Gorman. The pistol was pointed toward Gorman more than Loughlin, because Muang Tzu regarded the mercenary as the more unstable of the two.

"Rice-slurping punk," Gorman hissed. "You shouldn't pull a gun on somebody unless you're ready to use it."

"I *am* prepared to use it, Mister Gorman," Muang Tzu assured him, a slight smile playing along his lips. "You forget I've been fighting the Communists in my country for last ten years. I've killed a number of men and none of them ever called me a 'rice-slurping punk.' I won't really mind shooting you if I feel I must."

"All right, Muang Tzu," Loughlin began, holding his hands at shoulder level. "You've got the advantage. What would you like us to do?"

"Remove your weapons, please," the Laotian replied. "I'll give them back to you when Mister Stone arrives."

"Like hell I will . . ." Gorman replied angrily.

"Relax, Gorman," Loughlin told him as he unbuckled his gunbelt and lowered it to the floor. "We'll get our weapons back so long as we behave."

"Kiss my ass, limey," the mercenary growled, but he unslung his Uzi and placed it on the floor. "That's as far as I go. I'm keepin' my Walther."

"That figures," Loughlin commented. "I thought you'd feel castrated without a gun. And you said *I* don't have any guts."

"Shit," Gorman sighed as he slipped off his shoulder holster rig. He lowered the Walther next to the Uzi. "I guess I ought to show a little goodwill so you guys don't think I'm a total asshole."

"Might be a little late for that," the Brit remarked. "But you'd be making a step in the right direction if you apologized to Muang Tzu and the Nguyens for your rude behavior and ethnic slurs."

"Sure," Gorman smiled. "How do I say 'I'm sorry' in Vietnamese?"

"Toy rat an han," Loughlin replied.

"Okay," Gorman nodded. He turned to face the middle-aged Asian couple who fearfully watched their three guests, uncertain of what was going on. *"Toy rat . . ."*

Gorman suddenly whirled and swung a hard right cross

to Loughlin's face. The punch knocked the Briton back against a window. Gorman thrust a boot into Loughlin's chest. The kick shoved him through the window. Glass and framework burst apart and Loughlin tumbled outside. He landed on the ground, the wind knocked from his lungs.

"Thua khang!" Mister Nguyen cried.

"Screw off, gook," the merc growled as he placed a foot on the window sill and ducked his head. "I got me a limey to stomp the shit outta!"

He jumped from the window, both feet aimed at Loughlin's chest. The murderous stomp might have crushed the Briton's breastbone and ribs, but Loughlin rolled aside. Gorman's boot heels struck the ground hard. Loughlin lashed out with a foot. The steel toe of his paratrooper boot hit the mercenary just below the right kidney.

Gorman groaned as the kick pitched him forward. Loughlin pushed with his hands and kicked forward to jump up from the ground. The Briton faced Gorman and assumed a Tai Kwon Do fighting stance.

The Nguyen property was surrounded by a tall bamboo fence. Loughlin and Gorman confronted each other in the usually peaceful setting of a simple garden, with small lilac bushes, a tiny crop of turnips and peppers, and a chicken coop. The birds squawked in terror as they fluttered against the wire enclosure which surrounded their pens.

"You're a little tougher than I figured, for an English fairy," Gorman snickered, fists poised for attack. "But when I'm through with you, you won't be cornholin' any more little boys in Picadilly Square."

Loughlin realized his opponent was trying to provoke him. He knew anger makes a man reckless. He ignored Gorman's remark and waited for the merc to make the next move. Gorman did not disappoint him.

The merc feinted a kick and threw a left jab at Loughlin's face. The Brit parried the punch with a palm, but Gorman quickly shifted his attack to a left hook which tagged Loughlin on the side of the jaw. Gorman drove a right upper cut to the Briton's stomach.

Loughlin grunted, but seemed to absorb the punishment. He bent an elbow and smashed it into Gorman's face. The tough ex-S.A.S. commando followed with a sweeping backfist which sent Gorman reeling into the bamboo fence.

The mercenary spat blood and swung a boot at Loughlin's groin. The Briton shifted a leg and took the kick on a thigh instead. Gorman slashed a cross-body karate chop at Loughlin's face. The merc's wrist struck Loughlin's forearm and the Briton stabbed the tips of rigid fingers under his opponent's rib cage.

Loughlin pumped a knee into Gorman's gut and slammed a solid right cross to the merc's jaw. Gorman stumbled and fell at the base of the lilac bushes. Loughlin waited for his opponent to get up. Gorman climbed to one knee, wiping blood from his mouth with his left hand.

"Shit, man," the merc said, gasping for breath. "I give already. I've had enough. Okay? Just let me . . ."

He suddenly swung his right arm and hurled a baseball-sized rock at the Briton's head. Loughlin ducked and the projectile sailed over head. Gorman quickly rose and swung a vicious kick at Loughlin, but the Briton hands snared his opponent's ankle. A sharp twist threw Gorman off-balance and sent him tumbling across the ground.

Gorman started to rise. Loughlin kicked him in the ribs and smashed the side of his hand between the guy's shoulder blades. Gorman fell on his face and moaned in dazed pain. Loughlin straddled his fallen opponent, placed a knee at the small of Gorman's spine, and grabbed the merc's hair. He pulled Gorman's head back and slipped a hand under the bastard's jaw.

"I ought to do the world a favor and break your bloody neck," Loughlin rapsed, breathing hard. "I still think you know more about that ambush at the Golden Butterfly last night. If I knew for sure you're as dirty as I think you are, I'd kill you right now."

"What the hell's going on here?" Mark Stone demanded as he marched into the garden. "Have you two gone nuts?"

Loughlin glanced up at his cohort and growled. "Give me a few minutes to work on him and I'll make this bastard answer a few questions about that bullet-throwing donnybrook we had last night."

"Let go of him," Stone snapped. "We've got enough shit on our hands without you two acting like a pair of snot-nosed kids who want to tussle during recess."

Reluctantly, Loughlin climbed off Gorman's back. He allowed the mercenary to get to his feet. Gorman weaved unsteadily on rubbery legs. He glared at Loughlin.

"When this mission is over..." he began.

"You two can punch each others' heads off after the mission if you want," Stone told them. "But until then, you'll save the fighting for the enemy. I don't want to have to break you two up again. Any fucking-around in the field I'll regard as an effort to undermine the mission. That means I might just put a bullet through the troublemaker's head."

"All right," Loughlin said with a nod. He turned to Gorman. "But you'd better stay clear of me, bloke. Don't open your mouth unless it's important. Don't get any closer to me than you have to unless we need you. And then you'd damn well better be there."

"Yes, sir," Gorman snapped off a mock salute. "Whatever his lordship wants."

Stone thrust a finger at Gorman's face. "Listen, pal. Get a handle on that temper and that mouth of yours. Last warning or you're out."

Gorman looked at the ground. "I'll do my job," he growled sullenly.

"And bear something else in mind, both of you," Stone continued. "You two had a fistfight right in front of Muang Tzu. He happens to be the leader of the Laotian freedom fighters we're gonna be working with. And I don't think your silly-ass stunt is the sort of thing that inspires confidence. We can't afford another incident like this."

"Don't worry," Gorman commented, as he rubbed his rib case. "I'm not eager for a rematch. I don't think anything's broken, but I might have a bruised rib or two. Mind if I go inside and check this out? Gotta take a piss anyway —I'd like to find out if I'm passing blood."

"Go ahead."

The merc entered the Nguyen house. Muang Tzu passed Gorman at the doorway. The Laotian stood back to avoid bumping into the surly mercenary, but he could not repress a smile when he noticed Gorman was staggering a bit. Muang Tzu stepped outside and joined Stone and Loughlin.

"Congratulations, Mister Loughlin," he declared. "You certainly gave that lout a proper thrashing."

"Gorman got in a couple of good licks himself," the Brit admitted. He carefully touched his sore jaw. "Son of a bitch isn't terribly skilled, but he's got a real talent for fighting dirty."

"Hey," Stone said sharply. "I'm not very happy with *either* of you guys. What's all this duke-it-out bullshit?"

"Mister Loughlin did not have much of a choice," Muang Tzu stated. "Gorman knocked him through that window and tried to stomp him to death. Nguyen and his wife saw this as well."

"Great," Stone muttered. "I bet they'll be really eager to let us use their home for a safehouse after this."

"Mark," Loughlin began. "I've said this before, but I've got to say it again. Gorman is bad news. Kick him off the mission *now*, before it's too late."

"I'd like to," Stone assured him. "but we've got to pull out today, as soon as possible. Hitting an armed P.O.W. base in the plateau region isn't going to be a cakewalk. We need the bastard."

"Maybe you're right," Loughlin allowed. "What did you learn from the visit to Coleman's 'secret headquarters' last night?"

"I learned that Hog's description of them as the Three Stooges was an insult to the memories of Larry, Moe, and Curly Joe," Stone replied with a shrug. "I'm not sure one way or the other. Naturally Coleman denies that he sent a hit team to try to off us, but he'd do that anyway, whether he sent them or not. My gut feeling is he's telling the truth."

"Could be those gunmen were after Gorman," Loughlin reminded Stone. "He didn't like the idea of risking his ass for a measly five grand, but he accepted the job anyway. Maybe that was because he wants to get out of Thailand for a while."

"He could pick safer ways to do that," Stone said with a shrug. "The Communists might have sent those guys after us last night, or Coleman is a better liar than I think he is. Even if Gorman's enemies are responsible, that won't make much difference after we get across the border into Laos."

"Rumors about Gorman's Golden Triangle connections mentioned an opium czar based in Laos," Loughlin commented.

"Nothing I can say is going to cheer you up, is it?" Stone snorted. "We've got a job to do. Let's just concentrate on that. Okay? Now, did An Khom come up with all the supplies for our mission?"

"Everything except the cloak," Loughlin answered.

"What cloak?" Stone asked with a puzzled expression.

"The cloak of invisibility we'll need to sneak across the bloody border into Laos with a cart full of guns and ammo."

"Don't worry. I've got a plan."

"And that's suppose to stop me from worrying?" Loughlin rolled his eyes toward the sky.

"*Chao ong Stone,*" Mister Nguyen called from the doorway. He stepped aside to let his wife emerge. She carried a bamboo tray with a tea pot and several cups. "*Ong thitt uong tra khong?*"

"*Thua co,*" Stone replied. "*Xin cam on ong lam lam, ong Nguyen.*"

"*Toy khong dam,*" Nguyen replied with a smile, pleased that Stone had accepted his invitation for tea.

* * *

Gorman heard the others chattering away in Vietnamese. God, he hated the sound of that language. Of course, he understood it to a degree, although he had pretended he didn't when Loughlin had been talking with Nguyen earlier. Gorman had found it advantageous to pretend to be ignorant when Asians spoke with each other or occidentals in their own language. He had learned many things which people had not wanted him to know that way.

Stone and his chums were going to have a tea party out in the garden, Gorman realized. Good. He wanted some time away from those assholes. Goddamn limey was going to pay for what he did to Leo Gorman, the mercenary thought with a sadistic smile. Nobody pounds on Leo Gorman and lives to brag about it.

Still, he knew he would have to be careful. Loughlin was a lot tougher than he thought, and Stone was probably even more dangerous than the Englishman. Gorman would have to watch himself around those guys. Stone might be a little idealistic and soft-hearted for his damn M.I.A.'s, but the ex-Green Beret was no fool and he could handle himself in a fight. Last night at the Golden Butterfly proved that.

The mercenary raised the receiver from the cradle of the Nguyen phone—an unusual item for a family in Southeast Asia—and dialed a Bangkok number by memory. The phone on the opposite end of the line rang twice. A voice answered with some phrase in Thai Gorman was not familiar with.

"This is Gorman," the merc said. "Let me talk to Tratt Budan."

"Tratt Budan?" the Thai at the opposite end of the line answered. He said something and passed the phone to another party.

"This is Tratt Budan," a familiar voice announced.

"It's me, Gorman."

"Hello, Leo," Tratt Budan began in a sickening sweet voice. "We missed you last night. Of course, there will be other opportunities."

"Hell, Tratt Budan," Gorman said. "I talked to Dao Thong last night. Didn't he tell you what I said?"

"Something about making it worth our while to let by-gones be bygones," Tratt Budan chuckled. "You're suppose to have some sort of deal to offer which will be worth a fortune if we agree to bury the hatchet—somewhere other than in your skull."

"Tell Khong Noh I'm leaving Thailand," Gorman insisted. "I'm going into Laos with a group of idiots who plan to rescue some American P.O.W.'s from a camp in the plateau area."

"You're going into Laos?" Tratt Budan laughed. "If the Communists don't kill you, Khong Noh surely will. I'm certain he appreciates you making revenge so easy for him."

"He doesn't want me dead," Gorman insisted. "I've got a plan which will make him a very rich man."

"He is already a very rich man," Tratt Budan replied.

"And he wants to be richer," the merc stated. "Now listen real close while I explain this, because I can only explain this once. I gotta talk quick before they catch me on the fuckin' phone."

"Who are 'they'?"

"Have you ever heard of a guy named Mark Stone?" Gorman asked. "Well, he's gonna help me with a scheme which is going to make us all very happy and wealthy."

"How can one be unhappy with wealth?" Tratt Budan said dryly. "All right, Leo. I'm listening."

Chapter Seven

The water buffalo slowly hauled the cart from the rice paddy. Three figures walked alongside the beast and its burden. They wore loose-fitting work clothes, cone-shaped hats made of woven rice reeds, and sandals. Stacks of palm leaves covered the back of the cart. The little group moved slowly through the four-foot high elephant grass. One man marched beside the buffalo, tapping it with a prodding stick. The other two shuffled along next to the cart, their backs arched and heads bowed as they leaned against walking staves of hard *take* bamboo. Long whisps of white hair extended from their chins.

"See," Stone whispered, turning his head to peer from the rim of his conical hat. "I told you it would work."

"It hasn't worked yet," Loughlin replied. He was playing the other old man. Strands of white hair were glued to his chin. Stone thought he looked like an English comic in a *Monty Python* skit, dressed up as Ho Chi Minh.

"We got across the border," Stone insisted. "We're in Laos and on our way to the plateau region. It's worked so far."

"We've avoided getting close to any patrols thus far,"

Loughlin muttered. "But if anybody gets a good look at us, neither of us are going to fool anyone that we're a pair of Laotian senior citizens."

"No, we won't," Stone had to admit. He'd been thinking how unconvincing Loughlin's disguise was, and he realized the Briton probably looked more like an elderly Asian than he did himself.

"Bloody right we won't," Loughlin snorted. "If we even straighten our backs we'll attract attention, because we're too damn tall."

"Not all Laotians are under five feet tall," Muang Tzu declared dryly as he continued to encourage the buffalo to keep moving.

"Don't pay too much attention to Terrance," Stone told the Laotian freedom fighter. "He always has to find something to bitch about. That's his nature."

"Well, I'm glad *you* think everything is ducky," Loughlin muttered. "Especially since we've got some company heading this way."

Two jeeps rolled across the rugged terrain and headed toward Stone's little group. The vehicles came to a halt and several uniformed troops jumped out and advanced on foot. Most wore fatigue uniforms and pith helmets. The majority wore sandals. In the Laotian armed forces, boots and shoes are still worn mostly by senior N.C.O.'s and officers. An officer with a cap bearing the red star and laurel symbol walked at the rear of the group. A single silver star on the shoulder board of his uniform labeled the officer as a second lieutenant.

The symbols of rank among Laotian and Vietnamese are strikingly different from those used by the United States military. Gold emblems are higher ranking than silver, exactly the opposite of the American armed forces. Every officer in the Vietnamese army above the rank of student officer wears stars on his shoulder boards. Stone remembered an occasion back in 1969 during the war when his team encountered a patrol of N.V.A. troops at the DMZ. Following the battle, a young paratrooper excitedly announced that they had killed a "goddamn three star general", but the slain N.V.A. officer was actually just a captain.

"*Suh bye di,*" Muang Tzu greeted as the Laotian soldiers approached. "*Chao suh-bye di bau?*"

The soldiers did not bother to reply. Three troopers formed a semicircle around the "peasants" and the cart. AK-47 assault rifles were pointed at the travelers. The Laotian lieutenant and three other soldiers drew closer to the "peasant" group.

"*Pouak-chao men-pi?*" the lieutenant demanded.

"I am Meo Nhung," Muang Tzu replied with a bow. "I am a farmer, sir. We are taking palm branches to my village to reinforce rooftops for the ordeal of the monsoon season."

"Indeed," the lieutenant said dryly. "And who are these two old men with you?"

"My grandfather and his brother, my great uncle," Muang Tzu stated. "I am afraid they are both a bit feebleminded. They must be looked after as one tends small children . . ."

"They're certainly not small," the lieutenant commented, gazing suspiciously at Stone and Loughlin. "Your family appears to feed them well. They look very strong and healthy for a pair of feebleminded old men."

"They still work in the fields every morning," Muang Tzu replied, although he realized how weak the explanation sounded even as he spoke.

"How about that, old ones?' the lieutenant inquired. "Do they work you two too hard?"

Stone's limited Laotian vocabulary did not allow him to translate and understand. Stone spoke fluent Vietnamese and Thai, but his Lao was not as good. Loughlin's Lao was even worse. Stone couldn't understand the Lieutenant but realized he had been asked a question. Of course, since Stone was suppose to be a senile grandfather, he would not be expected to understand everything anyway.

"Pouk-how-pi?" Stone asked in an unsteady, reedy voice. He hoped the lieutenant would not notice how terrible Stone's accent was.

"No you may not go now," the officer snapped. "Bring them closer. I want a better look at these two. And search the cart."

Two soliders approached Stone and Loughlin while another trooper moved to the cart. The lieutenant placed a hand on his holstered sidearm. There were also three other soldiers covering the "peasants" and two more who had remained at the jeeps. It was a dirty situation and it wasn't going to get any cleaner.

Stone suddenly lashed out with his walking stave. The hard wood pole slammed into the barrel of the AK-47 of the closest soldier. The bow knocked the rifle from the trooper's grasp. Stone followed with a rapid backhand sweep and smashed the stave across the face of the startled solider. The Laotian trooper fell to the ground and Stone dropped the pole to draw his Beretta 93-R from under his shirt.

Loughlin also went into action. He swung his stave in a *bojutsu* stroke similar to a standard military butt-stroke with a rifle. The pole struck another Kalashnikov from the hands of a Laotian soldier. Loughlin quickly thrust the end of his fighting stick into the soldier's throat. The Laotian staggered and fell, his windpipe crushed. Loughlin reached under his shirt for the .45 Colt hidden there.

The Laotian lieutenant dragged his Makarov pistol from leather, but Muang Tzu had already lunged forward. The freedom fighter grabbed the officer's wrist and shoved the Makarov away. The pistol barked as Muang Tzu delivered a heel of the palm blow to the side of the lieutenant's jaw. He bent his elbow and slammed it into the officer's skull. The blow struck the temple and caved in part of the Laotian commander's skull. He was dead in an instant.

Palm leaves flew from the back of the cart. Leo Gorman suddenly emerged, his Uzi submachine gun in his fists.

The mercenary pointed his weapon at the surprised face of a Laotian soldier. He smiled as he squeezed the trigger. A three round burst of parabellum lead crashed through the trooper's face and exploded his skull.

A soldier raised his AK-47, but Stone's Beretta snarled before the man could trigger the Kalashnikov. A trio of 9mm slugs drilled into the chest of the trooper. Another Laotian soldier fell dead, but one of his comrades quickly aimed his rifle at Stone.

Loughlin saw the Asian gunman about to waste his friend. The ex-S.A.S. commando fired his Colt pistol twice. Two .45 rounds slammed into the upper torso of the soldier. The impact of the heavy hardball slugs kicked the man off his feet and into oblivion.

Another solider opened fire with his AK-47. The buffalo bellowed in agony as half a dozen 7.62mm rounds tore into its thick hide. Muang Tzu had dropped to one knee and drawn a .45 autoloader form beneath his shirt. The freedom fighter aimed the pistol with both hands and triggered a deadly .230 grain missile which punched the trooper in the intestines. The soldier cried out, dropped his Kalashnikov, and doubled up to receive another .45 slug through the top of his pith helmet. The thin metal hardly slowed down the bullet as it split his skull and burrowed into the man's brain.

Only two soliders remained, stationed by the Laotian army jeeps. One trooper reached for a field radio to call reinforcements while his comrade aimed an AK-47 at Stone's group and opened fire. Bullets spewed dust near Stone's feet. A couple rounds splintered wood from the frame of the cart, but none found human flesh.

Stone raised his Beretta and triggered a three round volley at the rifleman. The guy's head recoiled violently, a mist of pink and gray brains spewing from his bullet-shattered forehead. Gorman's Uzi pelted the last soldier with a vicious spray of 9mm devastation. The soldier's body jerked wildly as half a dozen bullets tore him apart.

The man's corpse tumbled from the army vehicle, taking the bullet-wrecked radio with him to the ground.

"Is that the lot of them?" Gorman asked, taking the spent magazine form his Uzi.

"Yeah," Stone confirmed. "But they might have managed to radio for help. There's no way of knowing how many more patrols might be in the area."

"Poor beast," Muang Tzu sighed as he gazed down at the wounded buffalo. The animal's legs had folded and it lay on its belly, wheezing from a punctured lung.

Muang Tzu aimed his .45 at the base of the buffalo's skull and fired a mercy round into the beast's brain.

"We'd better get the hell out of here," Loughlin advised.

"*Stone!*" Gorman shouted, drawing his Walther P-5 from shoulder leather. He aimed the pistol at the ex-Green Beret.

Stone instinctively dove to the ground. A Laotian soldier had been poised behind him with a bayonet held ready. Gorman's Walther snarled twice and the trooper's chest popped two scarlet spiders. The man toppled backward, twitched briefly and died.

"Guess you didn't hit him hard enough the first time, Stone," Gorman remarked with a grin. "Don't worry. I made up for it."

"I owe you one, Gorman," Stone declared. "Thanks."

"Goes with the turf, pal," the mercenary said with a shrug. "We could take the jeeps and travel in comfort for a while."

"And the sound of the engines would alert enemy troops a mile away," Stone said, shaking his head. "No. We'll have to keep going on foot."

"The terrain gets pretty rough," Muang Tzu commented. "Thick tropical rain forest. Very difficult."

"That's in our favor," Stone remarked. "If it's difficult for us, it'll be difficult for the enemy. Less likelihood of meeting another patrol."

"Precisely why the rest of my band will meet us there,"

the freedom fighter said with a smile. "There is no such thing as a safe place in Laos, but this will be safer than most."

"There is no such thing as a safe place anywhere, my friend," Stone replied. "Except, perhaps, the grave."

Khong Noh was the chief enforcer of the largest opium producers and distributors in Southeast Asia. The governments of Laos and Vietnam knew all about Khong Noh and his business. In fact, the state got a healthy piece of the financial pie. Khong Noh was a realist. He knew that Communists hated capitalism, but they love capital. As long as the leaders at Vientiane and Hanoi made a profit, they would allow Khong Noh to stay in business.

He was a bandit and he never claimed to be anything else. He committed every conceivable crime that offered a profit. Khong Noh made no apologies for his life.

"So Gorman had the nerve to tell Tratt Budan to contact me," Khong Noh mused, tapping the tips of his long fingers together as he leaned back in a throne-like bronze and velvet armchair. "That American is a bit braver than I thought he was. He's also far more stupid."

"What do you think Gorman meant by his claim that he could make a fortune with Mark Stone?" Ban Xiang inquired. A stocky, well-muscled man, Ban Xiang was the bandit chief's second-in-command.

"Mark Stone has become something of a legend," Khong Noh replied, as he removed a glass stopper from a crystal brandy decanter. "The Laotian and Vietnamese governments would be willing to pay quite a handsome sum for Mark Stone's head."

"Do you think Gorman is really traveling with this man?" Ban Xiang inquired. "Gorman doesn't care about American M.I.A.'s or P.O.W. camps in Laos. Why would he accept a dangerous mission with Stone?"

"Gorman has betrayed us, Ban Xiang," the bandit chief said with a smile. "Where can he go? To run he'll need money. He knows now that we'll find him if he stays in

Bangkok. If he flees to Hong Kong or Taiwan, my friends in the Triad would track him down. He'll need more money to go to Europe or the United States. It would make things difficult, but we might catch up to him eventually."

"So coming to Laos seems totally absurd," Ban Xiang said, more confused than ever.

"Not really," Khong Noh chuckled. "Gorman is trying to get in my good graces. He wants us to forgive and forget, and he thinks he can do that by offering us Mark Stone."

"He's insane," Ban Xiang said. "The Laotian army will kill him before he ever reaches that P.O.W. camp at the *Plateau*. Even if he makes it, the camp guards will certainly kill him."

"If we were talking about Gorman by himself, I'd agree," Khong Noh said thoughtfully. "But Stone is another matter. He's been slipping into Laos and Vietnam for over a year. He's rescued quite a number of American P.O.W.'s and successfully smuggled them back to Thailand and eventually back to the United States. I won't count on him failing."

"Shouldn't we stop them before they reach the P.O.W. camp?" Ban Xiang asked.

"Certainly not," Khong Noh replied with a smile. "Let them try. If they fail to rescue the prisoners, the soldiers will kill Gorman for us. If they manage to break the P.O.W.'s out of the camp, then we'll take care of the situation. Perhaps we can capture Stone alive. If not, the P.O.W.'s will be just as valuable."

"The prisoners?" Ban Xiang frowned.

"The Laotian government would be pleased with me if I return their precious American captives," Khong Noh explained. "Have you ever wondered why the Communists bother to keep those ragged, half-dead American prisoners long after the end of the war? They certainly have no shortage of slave labor. Holding P.O.W.'s illegally would bring international condemnation from the rest of the world if this fact became known. So why do they still keep them?"

"I don't know," Ban Xiang admitted with a shrug.

"So they can parade their soldiers past the tiger cages and point to the animals in the zoo," Khong Noh explained. "Then they can say, 'look at what we've done to the Americans. We've treated them like beasts and no one has dared to make us release them. See how impotent the Americans really are?' That is the reason, my friend. That is why the Communists will gladly pay us to return their P.O.W.'s—if, of course, we manage to confiscate them from Stone and his companions."

"And what about Gorman?" the bandit chief inquired.

"He wants a deal," Khong Noh smiled thinly. "He wants us to go easy on him. Very well. We'll make a deal. We'll kill Gorman quickly, with a minimum of suffering."

Chapter Eight

The tropical rain forests of Southeast Asia always brought back thousands of memories for Mark Stone. Fourteen years ago, when he first came to Vietnam, he had been full of the energy and idealism of youth. He never expected Vietnam to be a free ride, but all his training in Special Forces hadn't prepared him for the harsh reality of the war.

He remembered the jungles. Every sound was threatening. At night, the drone of birds, insect and animals made him uneasy—until he came to see them as friends calling comfortingly from the darkness. When the animal life was silent, it meant his friends were warning him that something unexpected had entered their territory.

Now, fourteen years and countless battles later, Stone was again creeping through a jungle, just as hostile as before, the enemies just as threatening. Once again he was part of a team, on a mission, but this time around, there was no place to run to. There was no chance of calling for air support or reinforcements. The war had never ended for Stone. The situation had gotten more difficult and danger-ous with every assignment he accepted. But now the missions were of his own choosing, and the risks were accepted willingly.

The jungles of Laos were not much different from those of Vietnam. The insects didn't seem as hostile, but perhaps Stone was now just used to the six-legged pests. A pair of hornbills watched from a tree branch, their heads tilted with mild interest as they gazed down at Stone and his companions. Intelligent birds resembling tucans, but with armor plating on their beaks, the hornbills sensed that the men offered no threat. They had clearly seen humans before and did not regard them as dangerous.

Stone's team pushed its way through dense bamboo and heavy vines. Chopping through the mess with machetes was too noisy. They pulled and pushed until they could find an opening, and slithered through to pull and push some more. They spent most of the day doing this. It was exhausting, monotonous work. All four men carried more than sixty pounds of gear which made the task more difficult. Finally, they clawed their way to a clearing and stumbled into an area where the jungle did not form a solid wall of resistance.

"Jesus Christ," Gorman muttered, as he slumped against a tree trunk and lowered his ass to the ground. "How much more of this shit do we have to go through, man?"

He unslung two AK-47 assault rifles and a CAR-15 and dumped them on the ground. He also carried his Uzi and a backpack full of rations, ammo, medical supplies and TA-50 gear. The mercenary took a pack of cigarettes from his pocket, considered lighting one and shrugged. Gorman put the smokes away and reached for his canteen instead.

"We do have not much further to go," Muang Tzu assured. The Laotian freedom fighter lowered his burden to the ground and sighed as he sat in a cross-legged position. "My friends should be very close now."

"I sure as shit hope so," Gorman snorted.

"Let's open up some C's and take a break," Stone announced. "No fire, but Gorman, you can light up a cigarette if you want. The trees are dense enough to conceal the smoke and the smell won't travel past the bamboo."

"That's okay," Gorman replied. "I don't think I can spare any breath anyhow. My lungs already feel like they're about to close shop and say 'fuck you.' I'll wait until we're outta this mess."

"I wonder if the Reds found that patrol we encountered back there," Terrance Loughlin mused. "They'll probably figure those soldiers were killed by guerrillas because we stripped their weapons and ammo."

"That's the idea," Stone replied as he dumped his burden and lowered himself to the ground. "Besides, Muang Tzu's people will need the extra firepower."

"I just wish we didn't have to carry it all ourselves," the Laotian freedom fighter confessed.

"Everybody better take some salt tablets," Stone advised.

"Bon appétit!" Loughlin muttered sourly.

A loud bird whistle sang out from the bamboo. Stone instantly reached for his CAR-15 and Loughlin grabbed his Kalashnikov. Muang Tzu gestured for them to relax and responded to the birdcall with an identical whistle. The Laotian smiled at his companions.

"It is all right," he assured them. "My friends have arrived."

Four figures materialized from the jungle. The Laotian guerrillas were clad in ragged clothing. Some wore mismatched uniforms taken from Communist troops. All but one man wore boots which suggested they had killed a lot of officers and senior N.C.O.'s over the years. The guy who still wore sandals probably did so by choice. All four men wore coolie hats and carried assault rifles of Russian, Chinese, and American design. Ammunition belts crisscrossed their chests, and knives hung from sheaths on their belts.

"*Suh bye di,*" a guerrilla greeted. "*Chao suh-bye-di bau?*"

"*Koy suh bye,*" Muang Tzu replied. He turned to Stone and Loughlin. "This is Loi Lihn, my lieutenant. He does not speak English, but he is fluent in Vietnamese and French. Very good man. Very brave and an excellent fighter."

"Toy rat mung duoc gap ong," Stone told Loi Lihn, saying he was pleased to meet the freedom fighter in fluent Vietnamese.

"Xinn cam on ong lam lam," Loi Lihn replied with a smile as he thanked Stone. "It is a pleasure to meet you as well. Are you the man we have heard of? The one who rescues American prisoners of war?"

"I do my best," Stone confirmed. "Muang Tzu has told me about you, Loi Lihn. I am honored to be working with you and I hope we shall regard each other as friends."

"I am certain that we shall," Loi Lihn assured him.

"I do not see Phou and Sing Nah," Muang Tzu remarked.

"They are dead," Loi Lihn explained grimly. "Killed two days ago when we encountered an enemy patrol. I see you've brought more weapons and ammunition. That is good because we are almost out of cartridges, and several of our weapons have been jamming when fired in full automatic mode."

"That won't be a problem now," Stone assured him. "You men help yourselves to guns and ammo. God knows, we're tired of hauling it around. Get rid of those Chinese Type 56 rifles or save them for emergencies. The Russian Kalashnikov's a better choice and most of the Commies here carry them. Easier to get parts and magazines that way."

"Good advice," Loi Lihn agreed. "Did you bring much ammunition for the rifles?"

"More than two thousand rounds," Loughlin replied, easily slipping into the conversation, conducted in Vietnamese. "And we've got the hernias to prove it."

"This is very good!" Loi Lihn declared. He turned to the other freedom fighters and told them the good news in Lao. Subdued murmurs revealed their pleasure with the information.

"We've also brought some grenades," Stone continued. "American made M-26 fragmentation grenades. We took some Soviet F-1 handgrenades from the dead soldiers, so there are a few of them as well. I guess you fellows are familiar with that brand of blaster?"

"Not as familiar as we hope to be," Loi Lihn remarked with a sly grin. "Most of our grenades have been crude devices we've made at do-it-yourself jungle factories. Tin containers with gunpowder, nails and needles for shrapnel, and a woven hair rope for a fuse."

"I've seen them," Stone said with a nod. "Any of your people familiar with crossbows?"

"Naturally," Muang Tzu said with surprise. "But I would have thought crossbows to be rather outdated weapons for your taste."

"Crossbow is still one of the best ways to take out a sentry," Stone replied. "Can't argue with success. I assume your men know how to make curare from the bark of certain plants."

"Of course," Muang Tzu confirmed. "We've been fighting the Communists for more than a decade. We've learned most of the dirty tricks of the trade over the years."

"Good," said Stone with a nod. "We'll see if we can't teach you a few more. For now, I think we should set up camp and post sentries. Everybody can probably do with some rest. I sure as hell could."

"Yes," Muang Tzu agreed. "The sun is setting and we should try to get some sleep while we can. However, we generally move about at night."

"We'll probably make better progress then," Stone agreed. "But we'll also have to move in daylight. Probably best if we favor the dense forest by day and try to move about in the open only after dark. We don't want to meet another patrol. If we hit any soldiers between here and the P.O.W. camp, the army will probably alert the camp commandant. If he suspects we're trying to rescue prisoners, the son of a bitch will be prepared for trouble. Hitting that base is going to be tough and it'll be a lot tougher if we're dealing with dug-in troops. They outnumber us pretty badly already. Without the element of surprise, we're out of luck."

"Right," Loughlin said with a nod. "And since they're already planning to pull out for the monsoon season, they might decide to leave early if they suspect trouble."

"Or worse," Stone said grimly. "The camp commandant might decide to simply kill the American P.O.W.'s if he thinks they're our main target. He might even order all prisoners murdered."

"Time is a problem no matter what," Muang Tzu commented. "They'll be moving the prisoners soon because of the monsoon. If they haven't already."

"True, but we won't do much good if we're exhausted," Stone said. "Let's get some rest and discuss tactics later. Fact is, anything we plan will have to be flexible enough to adjust to the circumstances we'll find at the camp."

"How much further before we reach the *Plateau des?*" Loughlin asked Muang Tzu.

"About forty kilometers," the freedom fighter answered. "But covering territory won't be easy. The terrain is difficult and we'll have to be careful about patrols.

"We'll have to risk it," Stone replied. "We'll try to reduce the danger, but the mission comes first. Regardless of the odds, I'm still going ahead, but I can't force any of you to stick out your neck if you choose not to."

"Do you think we'll back down because of the odds?" Muang Tzu demanded, a trace of anger in his tone.

"No, I don't," Stone assured him with a gentle smile. "I guess I said that crap for my own sake. Reassurance that I'm not going to be responsible for any lost lives during this mission."

"No one will hold you responsible, Mister Stone," Loi Lihn said. "And you don't know that any of us will be killed during this mission."

"Call me Mark," Stone invited. "And I have to accept a certain degree of responsibility. So do you and Muang Tzu.

When a man accepts a role of leadership, he also accepts responsibility for those he leads."

"You're right," Muang Tzu agreed grimly. "Everytime one of my men is killed in action, I die a little bit myself."

"I know the feeling," Stone assured him. "Unfortunately, we'll probably experience it again before this mission is over. There are bound to be casualties. For that matter, there's a pretty good chance none of us will get out of this alive."

"At least we'll die in good company," Loughlin commented sourly.

Chapter Nine

Coleman frowned. He gazed into the mirror, vainly attempting to adjust his toupee. "Goddamn Stone ruined this hairpiece!"

He continued combing the mangy black bangs over his forehead. "Who the hell does he think he is? Charging into a Company operations headquarters!"

"Uh . . . How much did that toupee cost, sir?" Donner inquired.

"I'm talking about an unwarranted assault on government agents of the United States of America while they are exercising their official duties for a federal agency," Coleman declared. He whirled away from the mirror to thrust an index finger at Donner. *"That's* what I'm talking about. That's the same as launching an attack on the United States of America! That son of a bitch Stone has gone too damn far this time and I'm going to put him out of business if I have to kill the bastard!"

"Yeah," Donner nodded. "But we haven't been able to find him yet. We've contacted all sorts of people who were supposed to know something about the guy, but so far we ain't got shit."

"We'll find him, by God," Coleman insisted, tossing his comb in the sink. "And when we do—"

"Alan!" Phil Lawson charged into the C.I.A. safehouse. "I finally got something on Stone—"

"Close the door and lock it!" Coleman snarled. "There's no need to tell everybody in Bangkok what we're doing here."

"Figure we should turn the radio on and turn up the volume in case the place is bugged?" Donner asked.

"Don't be ridiculous," Coleman snorted. The C.I.A. case officer took a pack of cigarettes from his shirt pocket and tapped a Benson & Hedges menthol from the container. "Okay, Phil. Tell me this earth-shaking news."

"Well, I was following up the theory that Stone must have connections with some big time gunrunners operating somewhere here in Thailand," Lawson began, searching his pockets until he found a small notepad. "Probably somebody based here in Bangkok because this is where they guy seems to spend most of his time. Some guys with connections to the anti-Communist groups in Laos told me that they heard Stone did a lot of business with some old fart named . . ." he consulted his notes. "An Khom."

"What's *his* story?" Coleman bristled.

"An Khom used to be pretty big in the arms business," Lawson explained. "They say he has principles. Wouldn't sell to Communists, terrorists, or dictatorships. Supposedly Diem tried to deal with the guy and An Khom told him to go to hell."

"Diem was on our side in 'Nam," Coleman growled. "Doesn't sound like this An Khom is an angel to me."

"Well, they say he was selling guns to genuine freedom fighters," Lawson said with a shrug. "Whatever that means. Anyway, he was selling and even giving away arms to the anti-Communist forces in Laos, Vietnam, and Cambodia, as recently as 1982. My contacts aren't sure if An Khom is still in the business or not. Maybe yes. Maybe no."

"Where can we find this gunrunner?" Coleman asked.

"I don't know for sure," Lawson admitted. "But I can find out."

"Then do it," Coleman said with a smile. "If Stone is still in Thailand, there's a pretty good chance he'll show up at this An Khom's place."

"What if he isn't in Thailand?" Donner inquired. "Maybe he's off hunting M.I.A.'s again."

"Then maybe he'll do us a favor and get himself killed this time," Coleman replied. "Sooner or later it'll happen. His luck is gonna run out some day even if we don't nail the bastard."

"Hell, Alan," Lawson shrugged. "Stone is still in Thailand and I bet we'll find him at An Khom's digs."

"Well, if we do that's great," Coleman stated. "And if he isn't there, we'll get this An Khom joker to tell us where the son of a bitch is. One thing's damn sure, we're not gonna be caught off-guard again. We're going to pay An Khom a little visit. And we're going to have plenty of muscle *and* firepower."

Ban Xiang found Khong Noh in the court yard practicing *tai chi chuan,* an ancient form of Chinese exercise and martial arts. The bandit chief moved slowly and gracefully, with perfect physical control. His hands pressed air as if pushing back a great weight. *Tai chi* develops mental concentration and spiritual strength as well as razor-sharp coordination.

Khong Noh raised a knee, turned slightly and slowly stretched out his leg to full length. He turned his head to face Ban Xiang. The rest of his body did not move. His leg remained extended and rigid.

"I apologize for disturbing you, Khong Noh," the lieutenant said with a bow. "I could come back later, but I thought you might wish to know what has happened so you can best decide what action should be taken."

"Very well," Khong Noh replied. His head moved, but the rest of his body seemed frozen in the same position. "Tell me what news is so vital, Ban Xiang."

"Two matters, Khong Noh," Ban Xiang began. "First, it has been reported by our sources within the army that a patrol of soldiers was wiped out near the Thai border. The official explanation is that guerrillas attacked the patrol."

"How large was this patrol?" Khong Noh inquired. He slowly revolved on a single foot, his other leg remained fully extended.

"Nine soldiers," Ban Xiang answered.

"Interesting," Khong Noh said thoughtfully. "Any word about the P.O.W. camp in the plateaus?"

"The troops are probably preparing to move the prisoners even as we speak," Ban Xiang replied. "But there is no evidence that the army suspects the attack on the patrol yesterday morning has anything to do with the P.O.W.'s."

"Perhaps they're right," Khong Noh sighed. He finally returned his airborne foot to the ground and stretched his arms overhead. The bandit chief gazed up at the pale dawn sky above. "A beautiful morning, is it not?"

"Yes," Ban Xiang agreed. "Very beautiful."

"So Mark Stone and Leo Gorman may be in Laos after all," the bandit leader mused. "It will be interesting to see if they can actually reach the camp and liberate any P.O.W.'s from their cages. Stone has done this sort of thing before. He might well succeed."

"With Gorman for an ally?" Ban Xiang remarked.

"Gorman is a professional mercenary and a skilled fighting man. No doubt, he'll fight alongside Stone and whoever else might be part of the group. Gorman doesn't mind killing Laotians. He'll kill anyone if it saves his hide. And he'll protect Stone from danger if necessary, just as he'll turn against Stone the moment that it is in his own best interest to do so."

"Treacherous dog," Ban Xiang hissed through clenched teeth. "Speaking of which, some of our men just arrived from Vietnam. They captured Thay Komgi near the Song River. The idiot apparently planned to take a boat to the Gulf of Tonkin and attempt to sail to China."

"No one that stupid should be allowed to live," the bandit chief declared. "He might find a woman willing to lie with him and sire another generation of mental defects."

"They brought Thay Komgi here," Ban Xiang announced. "We thought you might wish to speak with him before he is executed."

"By all means," Khong Noh said with a nod.

Ban Xiang turned to an archway and clapped his hands. Two bandits stepped forward, dragging a battered and bloodied figure into the courtyard. Thay Komgi's wrists and ankles were chained together. His face was covered with bruises and welts. One eye had swollen shut, but the other stared at Khong Noh with unfettered terror.

"What a pleasure it is to see you again, Thay Komgi," Khong Noh remarked as he approached the shackled figure. "For the last time."

"I did not betray you, Khong Noh," the terrified prisoner declared in a trembling voice. "Gorman betrayed you, not I!"

"You and Gorman stole twenty kilos of opium from a syndicate with which I had a contract," the bandit chief hissed. "You were supposed to protect the syndicate dealers and discourage others from interfering with their trade with the locals. Instead, you two cut the throats of our employers and you took the opium, planning to sell it for your own profit. That was stupid."

"Gorman did it!" Thay Komgi insisted. "How could I stop him? He had a gun—"

"Gorman needed someone who spoke English as well as Lao," Khong Noh declared. "That American pig could not get any connections in this country or anywhere else here without your help. Of course, the opium didn't do either of you any good because you had to throw it in a river when the soldiers stopped you."

"That was Gorman," Thay Komgi told him. "The man is insane! He pulled a gun on the soldiers and shot them down! When he ran away, I did not go with him."

"Because you assumed Gorman would immediately be hunted down and killed," Khong Noh said. "Who would have thought a white man would have managed to get to Thailand. But Gorman succeeded, although I will soon settle with him as well. You chose to flee in the opposite direction, to Vietnam. You thought we wouldn't look for you there. Once again you were wrong."

"Please, Khong Noh," Thay Komgi pleaded. "Give me another chance . . ."

"I'll give you one final chance, you lying filth," Khong Noh said with a nod. "Take the chains off him. I trust he has no broken bones or any serious internal injuries?"

"Nothing serious, Khong Noh," Ban Xiang said with a shrug.

"I hope not," Khong Noh replied. "I want him to have as much a chance as possible. I am a man of my word. And I give my word now, if you defeat me in open hand combat, Thay Komgi, you may leave this place unharmed."

"What if I lose?" Thay Komgi asked as the last shackle was removed from his ankles.

"Then you'll be dead," Khong Noh answered with a smile.

The others stepped back as Khong Noh and Thay Komgi squared off. The bandit chief assumed a 'horse stance', feet shoulder width apart, body turned sideways to present a narrow target. Thay Komgi breathed deeply, through his nose and out his mouth. He placed his palms together and held them to his forehead as he tried to will the *chi* to flow within his body, the mental and spiritual strength beyond flesh which bonds mind, body and soul together.

"Whenever you're ready, traitor," Khong Noh invited.

Thay Komgi suddenly flashed his hands in twin arches and snapped a kick for Khong Noh's groin. The bandit chief blocked the attack with a palm stroke to his opponent's ankle. His hand rose and backhanded Thay Komgi's right arm, sweeping it aside to expose the man's right side to attack.

Khong Noh thrust the stiffened fingers of his other hand

into the cluster of nerves under Thay Komgi's right arm. The traitor cried out and staggered backward. His right arm trembled as he clamped his left hand to his pain-laced armpit. Khong Noh whirled sharply and thrust a hard rear kick to his opponent's abdomen. Thay Komgi folded with a groan and Khong Noh slashed a "foot sword" to his face. The edge of the bandit chief's slipper-clad foot smashed into the prisoner's cheekbone.

Thay Komgi fell to the pavement. He rolled and came to his hands and knees. Slowly, Thay Komgi rose on quivering legs. He shook his head and tried to regain his *chi* by breath control. Khong Noh calmly waited for his opponent to launch the next attack.

"Come now," the bandit leader taunted. "You can do better than that, can't you?"

Thay Komgi shouted a wild war cry and lunged forward. He tried a short kick, a feint followed by a high kick aimed at Khong Noh's face. The bandit chief shuffled backward, avoiding the flashing feet of his opponent. Thay Komgi thrust a ram's head punch for Khong Noh's solar plexus. A praying mantis block parried the punch and pulled Thay Komgi off balance.

Khong Noh slashed the side of his hand to Thay Komgi's neck and kicked him in the chest, his heel striking sternum bone forcibly. Thay Komgi tumbled again. Khong Noh folded his arms on his chest and watched his opponent crawl to a kneeling position.

"Get up," the bandit chief ordered.

Thay Komgi dragged himself to his feet. Several bruises and welts had split open. Blood oozed from his face as he staggered forward. Crimson drool bubbled from his lips, yet Thay Komgi made one last desperate effort to survive. He lunged at Khong Noh and swung both fists at his tormentor's torso.

Khong Noh's hands struck like twin axe blades. He chopped Thay Komgi's arms aside and instantly struck out with a two-finger thrust aimed at Thay Komgi's face. The prisoner screamed and stumbled back as blood poured from the man's eyesockets. Khong Noh poised his hand in a spearhand formation. A glob of Thay Komgi's right eyeball still clung to the bandit leader's fingernail.

Khong Noh launched his final stroke. The tips of his fingers stuck Thay Komgi's solar plexus. His hand stabbed upward, driving terrific force into Thay Komgi's chest cavity. The man's heart ruptured. Thay Komgi collapsed to the pavement and died.

"That takes care of one debt," Khong Noh said with a satisfied nod. "Now let's see about dealing with another."

Chapter Ten

A Lao army helicopter appeared on the horizon. Stone and his group heard the chopper before they saw it. The great rotor blades of a 'coptor make an unmistakable sound—like a chainsaw backed by thunder. Stone and his team plunged into a bed of dense ferns as the chopper flew overhead.

Stone peered up at the aircraft between the green, spiny leaves. It was an American make, a Huey Cobra. He had seen hundreds of Hueys in 'Nam during the war. A Cobra gunship had once been a comforting sight. Air support called in to help American ground troops. Salvation from the sky with mounted machine guns.

But the Huey which hovered above him no longer belonged to friendly forces. It was one of the many hundreds of American aircraft left in Southeast Asia after U.S. involvement in Vietnam ended. The Huey was piloted by Laotian airmen, or possibly Russian "advisors". The helicoptor would bring no salvation for Stone and his band of warriors. It would offer them nothing but death and mutilation.

"It's moving away," Loughlin remarked. "Heading northwest. Opposite direction from ours. Thank God."

"Are helicoptor patrols common in this area?" Stone turned to Muang Tzu and the four Laotian freedom fighters.

"They fly over from time to time," Muang Tzu replied. "Not often. There is no definite schedule, the same as the patrols in jeeps and trucks. Of course, one can not be certain of schedules. The Communists change the hours of patrols from time to time, and not all the watch commands follow orders. The Communists try to make everyone live as if they are ants in a colony, but Laotians are still individuals, and individuals change their minds about virtually everything."

"That's a fact," Loughlin smiled. "I once knew a bishop who changed his mind a bit. Last I heard he was running a whorehouse in Liverpool."

"Right now I'm more concerned about that chopper," Stone remarked. "If they were looking for us, they have a pretty good idea where we're heading."

"Which means we might find a nasty reception committee waiting for us at the P.O.W. camp," the Briton said grimly.

"This is a stinking mess, but it could be worse," Gorman muttered.

"How's that?" Stone asked. "We could all do with some optimism right now."

"Well," the mercenary began as he glanced at his wristwatch. "It's past fourteen-hundred hours, right? Now, we've been on the march since before daybreak and we haven't come across a single patrol since those fuckers at the border yesterday."

"Good point," Stone agreed. "If they were looking for us and figured we were heading toward *Plateau des* and the camp they'd probably send out ground patrols, not just one chopper. Helicoptors are great, if the trees and brush don't conceal most of the ground below. Besides, one helicopter by itself isn't much use in searching out infiltrators."

"One gunship can blast the hell out of a company of ground troops," Loughlin remarked. "Maybe they figure they don't need more than that."

"Ever hear of rocket launchers?" Gorman smiled. "You can take out one of those whirlybirds with one shot with a good Red Eye rocket. One of those heatseekers would take that birdie out with no sweat. Too bad we didn't get somethin' like that for the mission."

"Well, we don't have anything like that," the Briton said, clearly annoyed with Gorman.

"But the goddamn Commies don't know that," the merc said with a shrug. "I figure they don't know we're here. They're probably fuckin' around the damn border looking for rebels, but they don't suspect we're planning to hit the P.O.W. camp."

"Well," Stone sighed. "We're going ahead anyway, so I hope Gorman is right. That Huey hasn't made another pass over us yet and he's had plenty of sky to turn around and try again. Like you said, Loughlin. That sucker's got enough firepower. No reason why he couldn't rake this area with machine gun fire if he suspected something was wrong here. Instead, he just took off."

"Guess we'll find out what we're in for when we get there," Loughlin said with a shrug.

"That's really profound, limey," Gorman snickered.

"Don't start this crap here," Stone cut him off sharply. He glanced from Gorman to Loughlin to make it clear his warning was for both of them. "There's too much at stake to risk because you guys have a personality problem."

"It's cool," Gorman promised, holding his hands up in mock surrender. "I just want to do the job, get out alive, and pick up my money when everything's finished."

"We'll be glad to see you fold up your cash, tuck it in your bloody pocket and skip on your greedy way," Loughlin muttered with disgust.

"I said *can it,*" Stone insisted. "Gorman's done okay

and that's all I care about. So far we've been lucky, but don't count on that lasting much longer."

"With that cheery note," Loughlin remarked. "I guess we'll get back to business."

"We've got to reach that P.O.W. camp by dusk," Stone growled. "I've got a bad feeling that time is running out fast."

The pit was eight feet deep and about ten feet in diameter, covered by bamboo bars and guarded by Laotian brutes who enjoyed urinating on the three American prisoners. Piggie, the fat Montagnard guard, often dumped garbage into the pit.

"Sanah nay oh," Piggie said with a laugh everytime he poured half rotten food and gnawed bones into the hole. He never seemed to tire of this joke.

The P.O.W.'s had wondered what the Montagnard had told them when he pelted the trio with garbage. One day a fellow prisoner, a Laotian who understood the Bru dialect, translated Piggie's joke.

"The food is good for you," was Piggie's big one liner.

For the last six months, the filthy pit was home base to the three Americans. And now, Piggie and Sergeant Phin watched the P.O.W.'s stagger from their hole. The guards exchanged glances and smiled. Together they moved forward and clubbed Lieutenant Nick Hall and Corporal Dwayne Franklin across the kidneys with their bamboo cudgels. The pair groaned and fell forward. Sergeant Jackson sprawled helplessly across the ground.

"You lazy American bastards want to lie around all day?" Phin demanded as he stepped forward and kicked Lt. Hall in the ribs. "We're in no mood for this sort of behavior!"

Piggie made a comment in Bru and stomped on the small of Sgt. Jackson's back. Weak and feverish from malaria, the N.C.O. moaned and feebly tried to crawl away from the guard's stomping boots. Piggie kicked Jackson in the ribs and flogged him with the bamboo pole.

"Son of a bitch!" rasped Franklin, as he angrily rose and lunged at the Bru sadist.

Piggie cried out with alarm when the lanky black man pounced on him. Both men fell to the ground. Franklin seized Piggie's bamboo baton and shoved it under the guard's throat. He pinned the Bru and pressed the club across his throat.

Sergeant Phin came to Piggie's rescue. He slammed his baton across Franklin's neck and shoulders. The corporal groaned, but held onto Piggie, determined to throttle the Bru. Phin clubbed Franklin again and kicked the black man in the face. Franklin tumbled to the ground, blood spilling from his split lips. Phin prepared to kick him again.

Hall crawled forward and seized Phin's ankle. He pulled with all the might his weakened body could muster. Phin screamed and fell. Other prisoners shouted encouragement to the Americans. A few tried to kick open the doors to their cages. Guards armed with AK-47s pointed their weapons at the Laotian and Vietnamese P.O.W.'s and the cheers ended abruptly.

A guard slugged Hall before he could crawl onto Phin's back. The officer fell dazed and curled himself into a ball to try to protect his head, groin, and kidneys from the boots which hammered him from three directions. Captain Luang ordered his men to stop. Guards stepped back from the battered and bloodied Americans. Piggie scurried away, rubbing his bruised throat while he gasped for air.

"You Americans disgust me," Cpt. Luang declared as he approached the P.O.W.'s. "We simply order you to move forward and you attempt to fight us."

"Guards . . . attacked . . . us," Hall replied, gulping breath into his lungs between each word.

"Liar!" the commandant snarled. He leaned forward and swatted the back of his hand across Hall's face. "We're leaving here. The time has come to head north to another camp before the monsoon begins. Why would my guards waste time by assaulting you three?"

"Because they're assholes," Franklin muttered in English as he wiped blood from his mouth with the palm of a hand.

"Shut up, ape," Luang snapped. "You know I don't like to hear you speak that accursed language. The three of you are fortunate we are in a hurry or I'd make you wear the Collar until your skin burns off."

"Sergeant Jackson is ill," Hall began. "He's too sick to survive a forced march . . ."

"Then he will die," Luang said with a shrug. "It doesn't bother me to watch Americans die. At one time there were six or seven of you scum. Don't you remember?"

"Seven," Hall confirmed grimly.

"Yes," the commandant nodded. "And one by one they died. I have yet to shed a tear over the death of an American butcher. You are all murderers, from a nation of murderers. If it was in my power, I would destroy every one of your kind. I would have every single man, woman and child in the United States sentenced to a slow and painful death."

"Captain Luang," Hall began. "I am truly sorry your family was killed during the war. But, the three of us aren't responsible. We were reconnaissance Marines, not bomber pilots. We didn't do it."

"Someone just like you did," Luang replied simply.

The commandant ordered his men to prepare the prisoners, and the tiger cages were unlocked. Other P.O.W.'s were herded into a cluster, and ordered to form a single line. The guards separated the Americans and shoved them into different parts of the line. Chains were attached. They would be linked together in a single file and forced to march north.

The P.O.W.'s had been through this ordeal before. A forced march is hard even on a healthy man. For a prisoner in poor condition, half-starved, weakened by malaria and frequent beatings, a forced march could well be fatal. Three of the original seven American P.O.W.'s had died during past marches. The prisoners were driven at a brisk pace, seldom allowed to rest, and given a bare minimum of food and water. If a man passed out, he was dragged by others chained to him. If the line slowed down because of this, guards would flog the P.O.W.'s and toss water on the unconscious man to revive him.

Sometimes they simply allowed a senseless prisoner to be dragged for hours. The line usually contained two or three corpses which had been dragged to death before the P.O.W.'s reached their destination. Some men suffered heart failure because their mistreated bodies could not bear the constant pain and stress of the ordeal. But the most common cause of death during a P.O.W. forced march was abuse by the guards. If a prisoner stumbled too often or otherwise slowed the progress of the line, guards would beat him with their clubs. Because they were linked to other P.O.W.'s, the victim could not be flogged across the back easily, and blows to the legs would merely make him stumble more often. So the guards generally beat "lazy stragglers" upon the head and shoulders or jabbed the ends of their sticks into the victim's gut and kidneys. The guards would kill a P.O.W. and allow the survivors to drag the corpse. This slowed the line, but the guards did not seem to care—if a dead man was responsible.

None of the P.O.W.'s were in good condition. The Americans received even worse treatment than the Laotian and Vietnamese prisoners. This had especially been true under Commandant Luang due to the captain's violent hatred of Americans. Lieutenant Hall was not certain he could endure another forced march. Dwayne Franklin was more or less in the same physical condition as Hall so his odds were about as good. Tim Jackson was another matter. The sickly N.C.O. would not survive a single day of a forced march.

"Oh, God," Franklin whispered. "Please . . ."

"Praying again?" Hall asked, annoyed with the corporal's obsession with what he considered to be a pipe dream of salvation.

"Don't fuck with me, Lieutenant," Franklin warned. "I

lost everything I got except hope. Don't try to take that too or I'll be all over your ass. Think I'm worried about being court-martialed for striking an officer?"

"No," Hall assured him. "I don't figure rank means shit after spending this much time. We're not officers and enlisted men anymore. We're not soldiers or Americans now. We're just prisoners of war in the shithole of the world. You hope all you want, Dwayne, and pray for your make-believe hero if it helps."

"You bet I will," Franklin nodded.

"While you're at it," Hall added. "You might ask the Almighty to send him real soon. Once they start the march, it might be too late."

Chapter Eleven

The sentries at the perimeter of the camp were watching the guards corral the prisoners when Stone and his team approached. The Laotian soldiers were preparing to move the prisoners. They were distracted with the task and didn't expect any trouble from the outside.

"This is better than we dared hope for," Loughlin whispered to Stone. The Briton clutched his AK-47, waiting for the signal for the attack to begin.

"Don't get overconfident," Stone replied softly. "Nothing is ever as easy as it looks. Muang Tzu?"

"Yes, Mark?" the leader of the Laotian freedom fighters whispered in response.

"Tell your men with the crossbows to get into position," Stone instructed. "They can take out the sentries silently from a greater distance. When we see the guards go down, the rest of us make our move."

Muang Tzu nodded in agreement and slipped away to contact his men. Stone and the others remained concealed within a dense bamboo forest at the base of Phou Xang mountain. They were less than a hundred yards from the

P.O.W. camp, close enough to count the number of Laotian soldiers stationed at the remote prison, and to see the guards about to chain the P.O.W.'s.

Christ, Stone thought. An hour later and the prisoners would have been gone. Still, he was not going to thank too many lucky stars too soon. They had found the camp. At least three American P.O.W.'s were still alive. But the prison guards could kill all three men with a single burst of automatic fire. Stone's group had to strike swiftly, and with superb precision if they wanted to save the prisoners.

He unsheathed his Beretta 93-R from its special holster rig. The silencer was already mounted to the barrel, ready for action. He eased the safety catch to the fire position. Stone also carried a CAR-15 assault weapon strapped to his shoulder. He glanced at Loughlin and tapped himself on the chest. The Briton understood that Stone intended to go first, using his silenced weapon to try to keep the assault as quiet as possible for as long as possible.

The first crossbow arrow hissed through the air. The projectile slammed into the chest of a sentry. The sound seemed very loud to Stone, but he had been expecting it and was listening closely for the sound. The sentry opened his mouth and his jaw moved as he tried to scream. Stone heard a slight groan and watched the guard collapse, the feathered shaft of the deathbolt protruding from the center of his chest.

Another crossbow missile hurtled from the forest. The second sentry received the deadly message between his shoulder blades. The soldier screamed as he stumbled forward. His arms flapped as if imitating a bird in flight, but he crashed face first to the ground. Other Laotians turned toward the man's cry of agony and saw their comrade fall.

"Damn," Stone rasped.

Advancing rapidly, the ex-Green Beret dropped to a crouch and ran through the tall grass at the edge of the camp. Two soldiers had rushed to the twitching form of the second sentry. Others tried to locate the hidden archer who had fired the crossbow. Voices alerted the rest of the camp to danger as someone noticed the body of the first sentry and shouted his discovery.

But no one saw Mark Stone.

He threw himself to the ground, assuming a prone position, both hands fisted around the Beretta. He aimed carefully and triggered the pistol.

A three round burst coughed from the muzzle of the silenced weapon. A trio of 9mm slugs plowed into the chest and bulging belly of Piggie. The Bru guard cried out as blood smeared his army shirt. The obese Montgnard fell on his wide rump and stared at his bullet-torn torso. He died with an expression of amazement frozen on his bloated face.

Sergeant Phin was standing three feet from Piggie when the Bru received his three holes in the chest. Phin jumped away, startled at the sight of his comrade's sudden death. He nearly staggered into the file of P.O.W.'s in his haste to get out of the line of fire.

"Oh, man!" Dwayne Franklin exclaimed. "It's really happenin'!"

Lieutenant Hall was equally amazed and took advantage of the situation immediately. He leaped onto Phin's back and grabbed the Laotian's throat. The guard struggled, stomping a boot heel into Hall's bare foot. He raised his bamboo club to try to swing it overhead at the American. Hall seized Phin's wrist to hold back the cudgel.

Franklin stepped in front of Phin and kicked the Laotian between the legs. The calloused ball of his foot slammed hard into Phin's testicles. The sergeant uttered a choked gasp. Franklin punched him in the face while Hall slid an arm around Phin's throat and placed a knee at the small of his back. Franklin's fists hammered the Laotian, striking faster and harder.

More than a decade of frustration, humiliation, and anger powered Dwayne Franklin. He hit Phin wildly, barely aiming the punches because he was eager to hit the bastard again and again. Blood spurted from Phin's nose and mouth. Hall yanked the bamboo club from Phin's hand. Franklin kept throwing punches.

Hall released Phin. The Laotian fell to the ground. Franklin followed him down, still slamming his fists into the guard's bloodied face and body. Hall gazed about the camp. Laotian soldiers dashed fearfully about, heads ducked low. Automatic fire erupted from the forest. Soldiers cried out and fell, blood oozing from bulletholes.

"How do you bastards like being on the receiving end for a change?" Hall said, his face beaming with satisfaction. "Tear 'em up!"

Two Laotian soldiers swung their Kalashnikov rifles toward the P.O.W.'s and opened fire. Hall dove to the ground. Something struck his right thigh. It felt as if he had been hit by a hammer and pierced by a red-hot needle simultaneously. Hall clenched his teeth as pain shot through his body like an electrical charge.

Howls of agony echoed from the line of P.O.W.'s as several rounds tore into Asian prisoners who failed to hit the dirt before the bullets raked the group. Other Laotian and Vietnamese prisoners managed to avoid the wave of high velocity slugs. Sergeant Jackson had already dropped to one knee, too weak to stand unsupported. Dwayne Franklin was still punching the motionless form of Sergeant Phin. Bullets sliced the air above the black man's head. Franklin sprawled across Phin's body. The Laotian sergeant was dead and had been long before Franklin stopped hitting him.

Stone returned his Beretta 93-R to shoulder leather and unslung his CAR-15. His strike force was already blasting the Laotian soldiers, but none of them had trained their weapons on the pair of soldiers who were trying to kill the prisoners. Stone aimed his rifle and squeezed the trigger.

A three round volley smashed into the upper back and neck of one gunman. The would-be executioner dropped his AK-47 and dropped lifeless to the ground. The other member of the firing squad tried to run for cover. Stone nailed him with another salvo of 5.56mm slugs. The soldier plunged to earth and slid four feet in the dirt. His body twitched slightly and died.

"Lieutenant!" Franklin cried as he scrambled to Hall's side. "You've been hit—"

"Yeah," Hall gasped, glancing at the crimson flow which poured from his wounded thigh. "I know."

"Hold on, Lieutenant!"

"Don't worry about me," Hall told him. "Grab a gun and start fighting, damn it. But keep your head down or you might get wasted by friendly fire."

"Yes *sir!*"

"And keep praying," Hall added with a strained smile. "Looks like you finally learned how to do it right."

Stone and his team closed in, weapons blazing as they advanced. He moved forward while Loughlin fired his AK-47 at the enemy to keep them busy. Leo Gorman was a veteran of dozens of firefights, and he knew the routine as well. The mercenary assisted Loughlin in setting down cover fire as the team advanced.

Muang Tzu and two Laotian freedom fighters attacked the base from the east while Loi Lihn and the last guerrilla struck from the west. They hit the soldiers with a deadly crossfire which tore bullets through the bodies of several prison guards. The soldiers returned fire. A man next to Muang Tzu dropped his weapon and covered his face with both hands. Blood oozed through his fingers as he fell. Muang Tzu realized there was nothing he could do for the wounded man at the present, so he kept going.

Stone reached the thatched huts which the soldiers used as barracks and headquarters. He yanked a pin from a grenade and hurled it through the open door of the barracks.

"*Lot loam kahn!*" a voice cried within the barracks.

Although someone had seen the grenade enter, no one managed to reach it in time to kick it back across the door. The explosion blew the flimsy roof off the hut and knocked down an entire wall. Stone peered inside, his CAR-15 held ready. Three or four dead Laotian troopers lay scattered across the interior. Their bodies had been torn up by the blast and half-buried by rubble. Two more Laotians were dazed and bloodied by the explosion. They tried to aim their weapons at Stone, but the vet's assault rifle snarled and both opponents fell before they could trigger a single round.

Gorman charged into the compound and fired his CAR-15 at a pair of Laotian soldiers who were trying to set up a mounted light machine gun. One guard dropped sideways, a trio of bullet holes punched in his chest. The other Laotian grabbed the frame of the machine gun and tried to aim the weapon at Gorman. The mercenary triggered another salvo and the Laotian's face exploded.

A volley of enemy fire screamed past Gorman. Two bullets slammed into the forearm stock of the merc's CAR. Black plastic burst apart, and the projectiles rang against the steel barrel. The impact ripped the rifle from Gorman's grasp. The mercenary whirled and fell to one knee, grabbing his Uzi in a single fluid movement. He raised the subgun and snapped off the safety.

The enemy trooper thought he had hit the American invader. He had not expected Gorman to spin around with another gun held ready. The guy failed to react swiftly enough as Gorman triggered his Uzi, and blasted a trio of 9mm rounds into the Laotian's chest. Another soldier fell in the battle and Gorman rose to continue the hunt.

Terrance Loughlin found two Soviet made ZIL-151 trucks parked at the rear of the camp. The big vehicles hauled up to three tons and the trucks were rugged enough to travel over any terrain short of an uphill climb on a mountain. Three Laotian soldiers had fled to the cover of the vehicles. They seemed uncertain whether to stay and fight, or try to flee in the trucks.

The ex-S.A.S. commando forced them to make a choice. He blasted the trio with 7.62mm projectiles from his AK-47. One Laotian collapsed, his torso riddled. The other two leaped for cover behind the nearest truck. They

fired back at the Brit with their own Kalashnikovs. Loughlin dropped to the ground, cursing, aware that he wasn't
covered from the enemy fire.

He braced the stock at his AK against his right shoulder
and triggered a long burst at the pair to keep them pinned
down, while his left hand pulled an M-26 grenade from his
belt. He continued to fire his poorly aimed salvo at the
enemy position as he hooked his right thumb into the ring
to the grenade pin. Yanking the pin free, he hurled the
M-26 in an awkward left-hand throw.

The grenade landed near the truck and rolled underneath
the vehicle. One soldier bolted away from the truck. He
ran into full view of Loughlin. The Briton tagged the guy
with a trio of slugs. The Laotian screamed and fell while
his comrade wiggled under the truck to try to kick the grenade back toward Loughlin.

The grenade exploded before the soldier's boot could
reach it. The blast ripped into the undercarriage of the vehicle. The Laotian was killed instantly, split in two from
crotch to forehead by the explosion. Metal and wood burst
apart. The fuel tank was ignited by the blast and flaming
gasoline spewed across the wreckage. Loughlin covered
his head and hoped he would not be bathed in flaming
petrol.

More burning gasoline splashed the second Russian
ZIL-151 truck. The flames licked across the cab of the
vehicle and poured through the cracks into the hood. A fuel
line ignited, and the tank to the second truck blew with the
force of two and a half sticks of dynamite. The ZIL-151
exploded and showered the area with more burning debris.

"Bloody hell," the Briton muttered sourly.

Captain Luang ignored the Makarov pistol on his hip
and gathered up an AK-47 from the lifeless hands of a slain
trooper. A rifle was better than a handgun in a firefight. He
glanced about at the destruction which surrounded him.
The barracks had been destroyed. The blaze at the rear of
the camp suggested the trucks were gone and the efforts to
set up a machinegun nest had been terminated before it

could really start. Dead Laotian soldiers littered the ground everywhere.

Luang had encountered rebel guerrilla forces in the past. They were clever fighters who struck with hit and run tactics, seldom attempting to launch a full-scale attack on a large number of troops. The assault on Luang's P.O.W. camp was not the style of the counterrevolutionary peasants. It had been professionally coordinated and swiftly executed, with ruthless efficiency. A burning gut-hatred in Luang's belly told him Americans were involved in the raid.

The commandant's fists tightened around the flame of the Kalashnikov. The damned Americans must have come for their fellow countrymen. Luang had never expected this. After more than a decade, someone had come to rescue the P.O.W.'s. Luang had been told the Americans had given up trying to find their M.I.A.'s, and that the cowards in the United States would never dare risk an international incident by invading Laos or Vietnam to save the unfortunate victims of an unpopular war.

Yet, Luang had also heard rumors about a man who defied the threats of both the Communist governments and his own country's policy concerning M.I.A.'s. These rumors had been spoken in whispers and laughed off as absurd, although news of numerous attacks on Laotian and Vietnamese camps added substance to these stories. Luang had dismissed such tales as propaganda, somehow slipped into the armed forces by the corrupt agents of the C.I.A. Perhaps those stories had been true after all.

Captain Luang didn't have time to think about it. The battle had lasted for less than two minutes, yet it already appeared that the camp defenses had been crushed. Luang realized he would die that day—but he vowed that the American prisoners would die before he did.

The commandant headed toward the area where he had ordered the P.O.W.'s to be assembled for the forced march. Several of the Laotian and Vietnamese prisoners were armed with weapons taken from slain guards. Some carried

AK's while others wielded bamboo clubs. They were staying low, firing at targets only when they were certain the
individuals were Laotian soldiers. Luang ignored the Asian
P.O.W.'s and scanned the line for the Americans.

At last he spotted two of them. Dwayne Franklin was
wrapping a makeshift bandage around the leg of Nick Hall.
Luang smiled. Apparently the white junior officer had been
wounded, and the black marine was tending the injury. The
pair were close together. Close enough to kill them both
with a single volley of an AK-47. Luang crept forward,
ducking behind a stack of metal water barrels. If he could
just get a little closer, the commandant was certain he
could take out the Americans before the invaders killed
him.

Loi Linh and another freedom fighter spotted Captain
Luang. Both Laotian rebels opened fire. The impact of the
bullets hurled Luang forward. He dropped his rifle and
tumbled away from the barrels. Fountains of water poured
from bulletholes in the metal skin of the barrels. Luang
heard the liquid splash and wondered if the sound was his
own blood gushing from his punctured flesh. The commandant could not breath and the pain in his upper back
nailed him to the ground.

He tried to call for help. His mouth opened and closed,
but no sound would come out. He tried to crawl. Neither
leg would move, and his left arm was a useless lump of
flesh and shattered bone. Shadows appeared. Shapes hovered over the commandant. He blinked his eyes and stared
up at the faces which gazed down at him.

"Bau!" Luang croaked when he recognized the features
of half a dozen P.O.W.'s who stood over him. *"No!"*

Dwayne Franklin, Nick Hall, and four Asian P.O.W.'s
did not respond with words. They raised bamboo clubs and
aimed the butt stocks of rifles at the cowering wounded
creature who had formerly been their jailer. Memories of
Luang's cruelties fueled their thirst for vengeance.

Luang covered his eyes with his right forearm as clubs
and gunstocks began to smash his body.

Chapter Twelve

Khong Noh peered through the lenses of his field glasses, watching columns of smoke rise from the forest near the base of Phou Xang mountain. He lowered his binoculars and turned to Ban Xiang.

"We were right about those gunshots. The smoke is coming from the area where the P.O.W. camp should be located."

"The army planned to move the prisoners to avoid the monsoon flooding the *Plateau*," Ban Xiang reminded him. "Perhaps they decided to execute the prisoners and burn the place down."

"No, my friend," Khong Noh assured his second in command. "The shooting lasted too long for that. It was a firefight, not a firing squad. And they did not torch the camp. We heard explosions, correct? Why blow something up when you can destroy it by simply lighting a match to it? No, Ban Xiang. The camp was attacked. Gorman told us the truth for a change . . . or at least a partial truth. I doubt that that mercenary bastard could utter a single sentence without lying about something."

"Do you honestly believe Mark Stone is with Gorman?"

"Gorman would not launch the raid on his own," Khong Noh replied. "He doesn't do anything unless someone pays him for his services. Mark Stone led the assault. Gorman isn't a strategist or a leader of men. He's a greedy barbarian, lacking any qualities of leadership. Stone, however, is a special kind of man. A warrior and a leader."

"You sound as if you admire him."

"I do," the bandit chief admitted. "Stone is a man of admirable qualities and considerable skill. I respect a worthy adversary. I rather hope he didn't get himself killed. Stone is worth far more to us alive than dead."

"The attack may have failed," Ben Xiang stated. "Captain Luang has more than twenty soldiers under his command. They may have wiped out Stone and his allies. Including that traitor Gorman."

"I know," Khong Noh agreed. "That's why we're not going to get any closer just yet. But, whoever won the battle, the victors will certainly leave the area. If the army won, Luang and his men will be headed north. If Stone and his group won, they'll move toward the Thai border."

"In the meantime we simply stay out of sight?" Ban Xiang inquired, clearly disappointed.

"That's right," Khong Noh confirmed. "Why make a task more difficult when a bit of patience can solve one's problems? We'll stay here and observe the area until we're certain of the outcome. If Stone's group failed, then we can return to the stronghold and celebrate the death of Gorman. However, if Stone and Gorman have rescued some American P.O.W.'s, then we'll have an opportunity to make a handsome profit and settle with Gorman at the same time. Revenge is sweet, my friend, but one never ignores an opportunity to make a large profit."

"I don't know if it is wise to try to sell the P.O.W.'s or Stone to the Laotian government," Ban Xiang said with a frown. "They might blame us for the attack on the camp."

"Not when we bring them Stone, a white man, in chains," Khong Noh assured him. "Besides, we may not sell them to the Laotian government. Not if the American C.I.A. is willing to pay more."

"The Americans?"

"Why not?" Khong Noh said with a shrug. "Stone is either working for the C.I.A. or defying it by sneaking into Laos and Vietnam without his government's sanction. Either way, "the Company" as they call themselves, will want Stone. If they want him badly enough to pay one million kip to give him to them, fine."

"One million kip?" Ban Xiang was startled. "Do you really think they'd agree to that?"

"Americans spend millions of dollars on all sorts of rubish," Khong Noh explained. "And a dollar is worth thirty or forty kip. A million kip is not a huge sum of money to Americans."

"Do you think the C.I.A. would pay us to deliver the P.O.W.'s as well?"

"Perhaps. But if they refuse, we'll simply sell the prisoners to the Laotian government. Either way, we'll make a good profit, Ban Xiang."

"And we'll punish that bastard Gorman," the lieutenant said with a smile. "I would like to kill him myself."

"Very well," Khong Noh declared. "When we find Gorman, you may kill him."

"Thank you, Khong Noh," Ban Xiang said with sincere appreciation. "I am honored that you offer this pleasure to me instead of claiming the right to execute the traitor personally."

"I killed Thay Komgi," the bandit leader said. "He was also a traitor and possibly worse than Gorman because Thay Komgi was a Laotian. One doesn't expect too much from Americans. Barbarians don't have a code of honor, but a fellow Laotian should have known better. Now let's get comfortable. We're going to be here for a while."

Khong Noh and his men were stationed on a ridge overlooking the plateau region. Numerous trees and rock formations concealed the bandits. They would light no fires and keep noise to a minimum, to avoid alerting their quarry.

Khong Noh and his force of fifty had traveled to the south without encountering trouble with the Laotian military. Khong Noh enjoyed government protection and carried papers which authorized him to travel throughout most of the country and allowed his people to carry automatic weapons. They were officially "special militiamen of the state".

They did not fear attack by Laotian freedom fighters or another band of outlaws similiar to themselves. Khong Noh's unit was well-armed and well-trained, more than a match for any ragtag bunch of rebels or bandits they might come upon. Khong Noh was also certain they could handle Mark Stone's little group of fighting men and a few half-dead P.O.W.'s who hadn't handled a weapon for more than ten years.

Khong Noh was confident of success, but he was a cautious man. He would wait until he was certain of victory before he made his move. He could afford to wait. After all, everything was in his favor.

Stone tore open a packet of instant coffee from a box of C-rations and poured it into the hot water in his canteen cup. He stirred the coffee and offered the dark liquid to Lieutenant Hall. The officer nodded his thanks and drank.

"Oh, God," he sighed. "I haven't had a cup of coffee for . . . Christ. I don't even know how many years I've been in this rat hole. More than ten. What year is it?"

"1986," Stone answered.

"I was captured in May, 1971," Hall said, his eyes misted with tears. "That's fifteen years, isn't it? I'm not even sure how to do simple arithmetic anymore . . ."

"Things start coming back to you after awhile," Stone promised. "You fellows held up pretty well compared to most P.O.W.'s I've seen. Some of them don't remember how to speak English."

"We kind'a worked at that," Hall said. "They kept us in

pits a lot. Three or four of us crammed into a hole not much bigger than a grave. We listened for the guard's footsteps and learned to talk while he was further away from the edge of the pit."

Stone nodded. He noticed Hall and Franklin spoke English more softly than Lao. They were used to whispering in their own language. Hall passed the cup to Franklin. The black man eagerly drank.

"Anybody for a cigarette?" Gorman invited, offering an open pack to the P.O.W.'s.

"Thanks, man," Franklin replied. He gladly took a cigarette. Gorman fired a lighter and held the flame for Franklin. He puffed the cigarette and rolled his eyes.

"Cigarettes and coffee," Frankin sighed. "I must'a died and gone to heaven."

"That's just the beginning, mate," Loughlin announced. The Briton knelt by a camp fire with several cans balanced on stones which surrounded the blaze. "I've just cooked up a delicious assortment of C-rations for you fellows. All those great army favorites are here. Pork and beans, chicken and dumplings, ham and eggs, an beefsteak. Can't swear to truth-in-advertising about this stuff, but that's what it says on the cans."

"Jesus, fella," Hall said, nearly choking on emotion. "You don't know how good that stuff sounds after the slop we've been forced to eat in this place."

"Try not to gulp your food down too fast," Stone warned. "Your stomachs aren't used to handling real food. Don't worry. There'll be more food later. Plenty more."

"Mister," Franklin began, tears welling up in his eyes. "I don't know how to thank you for . . . for . . ."

"It's okay," Stone said gently. "I was in a tiger cage for a while myself. The worst part is over now."

"Look," Loughlin said as he unwrapped some syringes. "I've got some vitamin injections here as well as some quinine and penicillin. Anybody allergic?"

Hall and Franklin shook their heads.

"How about Jackson?" Loughlin asked.

"Not that I know of," Hall answered. "He's in pretty bad shape. If he doesn't get some medical attention, he'll die anyway."

"Have to take the risk then," the Briton agreed. "Looks like malaria. Some quinine and penicilin could do wonders for the chap."

"How about the lieutenant's leg?" Stone asked.

"Bullet went clean through," Loughlin replied. "That's good. No major veins or arteries were damaged and that's even better. But, there's probably a lot of damage done to muscle tissue. I've done what I can for now. Disinfected and bandaged, all that. He'll need a real doctor when we get back to Thailand."

"We'll need a stretcher," Stone commented.

"I can walk," Hall declared. "Give me a crutch of some sort . . ."

"Don't be macho," Stone replied. "You can use a crutch if we can't carry you for some reason."

"Jackson needs a stretcher more than I do," Hall insisted.

"You both need stretchers," Gorman announced. "We can make a couple of stretchers easily, by using ponchos from our TA-50 gear attached to poles. You know that trick they teach in Basic? Just slide two poles in the slots of the poncho and you've got yourself a homemade stretcher."

"How about getting the poles while I check on our Laotian friends, Leo?" Stone inquired.

"Sure," Gorman grinned. "You decided to call me by my first name."

"If you don't mind," Stone replied. "I had some reservations about taking you on this mission, Leo."

"Me too," Loughlin added. "But we were wrong about you, mate."

"How's that?" Gorman asked, folding his arms on his chest.

"You handled yourself like a pro everytime we got in a scrap," Stone told the mercenary. "I'll see if I can't manage to pay you a bonus when we get back to Bangkok."

"And I'd like to shake hands and be friends," Loughlin confessed, although a trace of bitterness still slipped into his tone. "Let's forget about our differences. After all, friends don't always have to agree with each other."

"Why not?" the mercenary said with a shrug as he offered his hand to Loughlin. "I gotta admit, I have a lot of respect for you guys too."

Loughlin and Gorman shook hands.

"Well, let's not get bloody mushy about this," Loughlin snorted. "We still have a lot of work to do."

"And we can't afford to hang around here much longer," Stone added. "No telling how many enemy troops might have seen the smoke from those burning trucks before we managed to put the fire out. It's still smouldering a bit."

"What can we do to help?" Franklin asked.

"Eat your dinner and let us take care of the rest," Loughlin answered. "You fellows need some nutrition to build up your strength before we pull out."

"That's an order," Stone added. "I'm going to check with Muang Tzu and see how the Asian P.O.W.'s are doing."

"Hey, Stone," Gorman called out. "I gotta tell you about something that . . ."

The mercenary stopped in mid-sentence and bit his lower lip as if forcing himself to shut up. Stone turned to face Gorman, confused by the merc's actions.

"What is it, Leo?" he asked.

"Uh . . . hell," Gorman replied with a nervous smile. "It's not important really. We'll talk about it later maybe."

"Okay," Stone agreed. "Let me know if you change your mind."

"Sure," Gorman replied, bobbing his head in a wooden manner.

Stone approached the Asians. Muang Tzu's group had given food and water to the former P.O.W.'s and administered medical treatment as best they could. Everyone was well-armed with weapons taken from slain Laotian soldiers. They had also removed boots, sandals, clothing, and headgear from the dead guard force.

"Everybody here looks a lot happier now," Stone remarked.

"Yes," Muang Tzu agreed. "The mission went well, although I grieve for Qui Thin, the fighter in my unit who was killed during the raid. Still, he died for what he believed in. And he did not die in vain. Our victory is indeed great."

"Mission isn't over yet, Muang Tzu," Stone reminded him. "And getting everybody across the Thai border won't be easy. We've got twenty-three men in our group now."

"No," Muang Tzu corrected. "We have two separate groups."

"Oh?" Stone gazed at the thin faces of the Asians who had been prisoners of the Laotian guards. "Have you talked about this?"

"Yes," the leader of the freedom fighters assured Stone. "We're not going to Thailand, Mark. Laos is our homeland. What would you do if your country had been taken over by Communists? Leave the country or stay and fight?"

"I'd probably do pretty much the same as you fellows are doing," Stone admitted. "Thanks for your help, Muang Tzu . . ."

"Don't misunderstand," the Laotian said with a smile. "I am going with you to the border. So is Xon Vapi, one of my best men. He understands about five-hundred words of English. We'll be able to communicate easier."

"Where are the rest of these men going?" Stone asked.

"Loi Lihn is taking them to the southeast," Muang Tzu answered. "There is a rebel group there with connections to similar anti-Communist movements in Vietnam. Some of these prisoners . . . or should I say ex-prisoners?"

"You should," Stone nodded.

"Indeed," Muang Tzu smiled. "Some of the ex-prisoners are Vietnamese. They wish to return to their country to fight the Communists there. We all have our duty. They must fight in Vietnam. I and my fellow Laotian brothers must fight here. You, my friend—you seem to have a war everywhere. Things are not so simple for you."

"Not complicated either," Stone assured him. "It's just my war has many battlefields, but it's still pretty much the same war."

"I understand," Muang Tzu said with a nod. "It is your duty, yes?"

"Yes," Stone replied. "You do understand, Muang Tzu."

Chapter Thirteen

An Ling carried a tray to the table as An Khom listened to his guest. Mister Nguyen spoke little English, but An Khom understood Vietnamese and several other languages. He had no trouble communicating with the refugee. An Ling placed the tray on the table and poured tea for her father and Mister Nguyen.

"Xin cam on ong lam lam," Nguyen said with a bow, thanking An Ling. "You are a most gracious host, An Khom."

"You are a friend of Mark Stone, and his friends are always welcome in my house, sir," An Khom assured him. "Now, please, tell me what bothers you. On the phone you said this matter was most urgent."

"I believe so," Nguyen replied. The middle-aged Vietnamese gathered up his teacup and took a quick gulp. "Today, the police came to my house. I live in Ubon, not far from the border with Laos."

"I know," An Khom nodded. "Mark has mentioned you in the past. You have been a loyal ally to him many times, Mister Nguyen."

"I will do anything to help him," Nguyen stated. "If

Mister Stone had not helped my wife and I, we would still be prisoners in Vietnam under the Communists. I owe him a debt which can never be repaid."

"Loyalty is a virtue of an honorable man," An Khom said. "Why did the police come to your home, sir?"

"It seems they wanted to question me about a phone call which was traced to my home in Ubon," Nguyen replied. "A phone call made to a man named Tratt Budan. He lives in Bangkok."

"I've heard of Tratt Budan," An Khom said grimly. "He is said to be connected with the Chinese Triad and the golden Triangle opium trade."

"That is what the police told me," Nguyen said with a nod. "They said they had electronic listening devices connected to the telephone line to Tratt Budan's home."

"A phone tap," An Khom commented.

"Yes," Nguyen confirmed. "But Tratt Budan used some sort of device to jumble his voice and the voice of the caller."

"A scrambler," An Khom explained.

"Yes," Nguyen nodd nodded. "The police could not understand what Tratt Budan and his caller discussed, but they were able to trace the call to my house."

"I assume you did not call this hoodlum," An Khom said. "But do you know who did?"

"Yes, I do," the Vietnamese declared. "I told the police there must have been some sort of mistake. That their tracing equipment must be malfunctioning. I think they believed me, but in truth I lied to them . . ."

"Please, Mister Nguyen," An Khom interrupted as gently as possible. "Who called Tratt Budan?"

"The man with Mark and Terrance," Nugyen answered. "The man they called Gorman. The rest of us had tea while Gorman was in the house. I saw him at the telephone. At the time, I thought I heard the sound of the receiver hastily put down, but I thought this was just my imagination— until now."

"Gorman and Tratt Budan," An Khom frowned. "So the

mercenary is connected with the opium trade. Did he call Tratt Budan just before the group left on their mission?"

"Yes," Nguyen nodded. "That is correct."

An Khom gazed down at his teacup as if hoping to find some reassurance there. He looked up and nodded.

"Thank you, Mister Nguyen," he announced. "You did the right thing to come to me."

"Is this serious?" Nguyen asked. "Is Mister Stone in danger?"

"He usually is," An Khom replied. "But this time the greatest threat might come from a man on his team."

"What can we do?" the Vietnamese asked desperately.

"I'm afraid there is nothing we can do except wait for Mark to return," An Khom declared. "And pray for his safety."

The Volkswagon minibus pulled up in front of Ah Khom's estate. Phillip Lawson emerged from the driver's side, an Ingram MAC-11 machinepistol in his fist. A silencer was attached to the barrel of the compact subgun. The back doors to the bus opened. Coleman, Donner, and two young Thai goons with rock hard faces, stepped from the vehicle. The C.I.A. case officer also carried a MAC-11, the .380 caliber "little brother" of the MAC-10. Donner held a Smith & Wesson M-76 submachine gun. All their automatic weapons were equipped with silencers.

The two Thai thugs were hired muscle. They were former soldiers who had never adjusted to civilian life. The pair sold their skills as thugs, bodyguards, and part time assassins to the highest bidder. They had no politics and nobody could hire them. Alan Coleman had decided the pair was ideal for taking on Mark Stone.

"Okay," Coleman began. "I want to remind you guys that we're only interested in getting Stone. Nobody else is supposed to be hurt."

"Why we not have machine guns?" one of the Thai hoods complained.

"I told you," Coleman answered. "I don't want any innocent bystanders hurt. I figure that's less apt to happen if you two aren't carrying automatic weapons."

"We not shoot just anyone," the Thai who spoke broken English insisted. "Just Max Rock."

"Mark Stone," Coleman corrected. "And don't draw your guns unless I tell you to."

"O-fuckin'-K," the Thai said with a wide grin.

"Great," Coleman turned to Donner and Lawson. "I'm not so sure it's a good idea to let you two have machine guns, either."

"Come on, Al," Lawson said. "We haven't done that bad. I found out about this An Khom joker, didn't I?"

"What do you want, Phil?" Coleman snapped. "A fuckin' medal?"

"How about a raise?" Lawson shrugged.

"Maybe we'll all get a raise if this works out," Coleman replied, working the bolt to his MAC-11. "Everybody ready?"

"Yeah," Keith Donner said, although he was not quite certain he really was.

"Okay," Coleman began. "Everybody fan out and . . ."

Suddenly, a large figure appeared from the rear of the minibus. A ham-sized fist hit Lawson between the shoulder blades. The blow propelled him into Coleman and one of the Thai flunkies. All three men tumbled to the ground. Ingram machinepistols fell from the Lawson and Coleman's grasp.

A well-placed boot kicked the MAC-11 from Donner's hands. The other Thai goon yanked a pistol from shoulder leather, but a whirling backfirst from the hulking stranger knocked the weapon from his fingers and sent the Thai reeling. The big man turned to face Lawson and the first Thai as they rose to their feet.

"You boys wanna fuck with somebody?" Hog Wiley announced. "Y'all fuck with me."

Lawson and the Thai reached for pistols inside jackets. Hog Wiley plunged forward and pumped both arms. His fists hit them in the chest and lifted them into the air. Both men fell to the ground. Donner reached for Hog, trying to grab the big man's shaggy head. Wiley caught an arm and pivoted to hurl Donner into the Volkswagon.

"Shee-it," Hog sneered as he hooked a hard left to Donner's jaw.

The second Thai hood launched himself at Hog and threw a high-boxer kick to Wiley's head. The big man spun around from the kick and the Thai swung another foot for Wiley's groin. Hog chopped the side of a hand across his opponent's ankle, breaking bone. The Thai cried out in pain. Hog stepped forward and hooked his left fist into the guy's kidney. Wiley followed up with a fierce right which knocked the man out cold.

Alan Coleman drew his snubnose .38 revolver, but he did not want to kill the huge bearded man who had attacked them. After all, the guy was not armed and he was only one man. A man who might know where they could find Mark Stone. Coleman held the handgun like a club and swung it at Hog's head. Wiley ducked under the swinging gun butt and slammed a forearm into Coleman's armpit. The C.I.A. officer's fist popped open and his .38 fell. Coleman staggered backward, clutching his numb arm.

Lawson rose from the ground, dragging a .357 Magnum from shoulder leather. Hog's hands streaked out before the agent could point the revolver. He seized Lawson's wrist and pulled the guy off balance. Hog shoved the C.I.A. man's forearm downward to break the radius and ulna bones across his bent knee. Lawson screamed and fell to all fours. He howled even louder when his palm struck the ground.

"Shut up, asshole," Wiley muttered as he hammered a fist into the nape of Lawson's neck and knocked the man unconscious.

The remaining Thai thug launched a roundhouse kick at Hog's face. Wiley's hands swung into the Thai's calf to block the kick as he stomped a boot to the man's other leg. The big guy's kick shattered his opponent's kneecap. The

Thai screamed and fell to the ground. Hog kicked him behind the ear to shut him up for a while.

Keith Donner displayed his stupidity by lunging at Hog
like a football player attempting a high tackle. Wiley
swung a hard uppercut and hit the moron under the jaw.
Donner's head bounced upward and Hog decked him with
a left hook. Donner went down for the count.

Hog Wiley turned to face Alan Coleman. The C.I.A.
case officer swung a right cross to Hog's jaw. Wiley's head
barely moved. Hog hit him back and knocked Coleman
five feet. The CIA man fell near one of the discarded M-11
machinepistols. He grabbed for the weapon, but Hog's big
boot caught the weapon and pinned it to the ground.

Wiley grabbed Coleman's hair and yanked the toupee
from the guy's bald head. Hog looked at the mangy black
hairpiece with surprise and tossed it aside.

"Wearin' a dead rat on your head?" Wiley bellowed.

Coleman tried a final desperate attack. He threw a fist at
Wiley's groin. Hog moved a leg and the C.I.A. man's
knuckles struck the thick muscle of Wiley's thigh. Hog
brought a clenched fist down on Coleman's bald skull.
Alan Coleman saw a burst of white light, followed by pitch
black.

"What's going on out here?" An Khom's voice called in
Thai as the old man cautiously approached.

"Just found me some varmints hangin' around the hen-
house," Wiley announced cheerfully.

"Hog," An Khom said said, blinking with surprise.
"You're back."

"Fuckin' A right," Wiley replied as he strolled forward.
"I'm all healed up and ready to rock'n roll like a son of a
bitch. Where's Mark and my favorite limey? Wanta get
together with 'em and do some serious goddamn partyin'."

"The party is already in progress," An Khom replied.
"And it might be more serious than usual."

Chapter Fourteen

Wiley tapped his thick fingers on the table top as An Khom told him about Stone's most recent mission to Laos and his apprehensions about Leo Gorman. The conversation with Mister Nguyen had confirmed his fears that Gorman was connected with the opium trade. Hog shook his shaggy head.

"Shit," he muttered. "I go away for a while and look what happens? Mark and Terry get hooked up with some shiteatin' fuck who peddles poppies for the Goldie Triangle. You know, that mother Gorman might've set 'em up for some kinda ambush."

"My fear exactly," An Khom said with a nod. "I don't suppose you would care for tea, Hog?"

"Fuck no," Wiley replied. "Not if you have somethin' stronger. I've had all the rabbit food and sissy drinks I can stand while I was lyin' in a hospital bed back in the States. I'd be right glad if you could give me somethin' with a little piss and viniger in it."

"Piss and viniger?" An Khom raised his eyebrows.

"Alcohol," Hog explained.

"That is what I hoped you meant," the old man nodded. He turned to An Ling. "Perhaps you would be good enough to bring our guest some brandy."

"Thanks," Hog said with a grin. "Now whereabouts did my buddies go with this Gorman asshole?"

"The plateaus," An Khom confirmed. "Near a mountain called the Phou Xang. That's where the P.O.W. camp is located."

"Some Laotian freedom fighters went with 'em," Hog mused. "Maybe they're okay. Maybe Gorman just called that Tratt ratt or whatever his name is because he owed the fucker money and was promisin' to pay it back."

"Do you believe that, Hog?" An Khom inquired doubtfully.

"Hell no," Wiley admitted. "But it sure sounded good for a minute. Could use a little encouragement, but I reckon tryin' to bullshit yourself is the high point of stupidity."

"Accepting reality is not always pleasant," An Khom agreed. "Yet it is the most fundamental form of wisdom."

"You're not shittin'," Wiley said with a nod. "Ain't no point in wringin' my hands over it."

"You may stay here tonight, Hog," An Khom told him.

"Much obliged," Wiley replied. "But I figure I'd best try to scare up some fellers to help me find this camp."

"Your brandy," An Ling announced, smiling at Hog as she placed a bottle and glass on the table.

"Thanks a bunch, hon," Wiley grinned. "I swear you look prettier every time I see you, An Ling."

"Thank you, Hog," she replied. "Are you going to try to help Mark in Laos?"

"I aim to," Hog confirmed.

"How do you intend to do this?" An Khom inquired.

"I'll have to find somebody who speaks Lao and knows the area," Wiley answered. "Any idea where I might start lookin'?"

"I heard from a representative of another group of Laotian freedom fighters this morning," the old man said. "They wish to get guns and ammunition, but they have little money and they've been unable to get any arms elsewhere. However, their leader, Viang Tha, is a former soldier. He was a helicopter pilot for the army, before he turned against the Communists."

"Sure this feller can be trusted?" Hog asked, pouring himself a generous portion of brandy.

"Yes," An Khom assured Wiley. "I'm familiar with one of the other men in the group. A man named Lan Nhung. They're a genuine group. However, there are only three of them here in Bangkok."

"Reckon you could arrange for me to meet these fellers tonight?" Hog asked, gulping his drink.

"It's nine p.m.," An Khom said, glancing at an antique wall clock. "I doubt that they're asleep, but in Bangkok . . . they could be anywhere."

"Tell me where they're stayin'," Hog suggested. "I'll start lookin' for 'em there. If they aren't at their rooms, I'll try the bars and whorehouses. That's probably where I'll find 'em."

"I think not," An Khom said. "These are dedicated fighting men."

"Show me a man who loves to fight and I'll show you a man who loves to fuck," Wiley replied.

The old man smiled. "Is there anything I can do to assist you?"

"Just try to contact anybody who can help us sneak across the border and make sure we've got enough guns and ammo," Hog answered. "Don't wanna cross into Laos with just our dicks in our hands."

"Naturally," An Khom agreed. "I'll check my files and get the names and current addresses of the Laotians and see if I can find any other information that will help."

"That'd be mighty good of you," Hog told him. "Good brandy too."

"Thank you," An Khom replied. "It's always pleasant when we have these little conversations. I always feel I learn something new. Even if I'm not always sure what it is."

"I know just what you mean," Hog assured him.

Mark Stone and Terrance Loughlin lowered the stretcher with Lieutenant Hall on it to the ground. Muang Tzu and Xon Vapi, the other Laotian freedom fighter with Stone's group, carried Sergeant Tim Jackson on another stretcher. Gorman and Corporal Franklin walked point, their weapons held ready. The Laotians placed Jackson on the ground and Loughlin knelt by the ex-P.O.W.

"How's he doing?" Stone asked, watching Loughlin check Jackson's pulse.

"Better,' the Briton answered. "His pulse is stronger and the swelling in infected areas seems to be less."

"Damn right," Jackson croaked hoarsely. "I . . . *Toi rat doi on.*"

"*Toi khong dam,*" Strong replied. He switched to Vietnamese. "Don't worry. English will come back to you after a while. The lieutenant told us how you could only whisper in your own language."

"I haven't done much talking for the last year or so," Jackson said. "Been sick all the time. Would have died long ago if the lieutenant and Dwayne hadn't kept me going."

"Hang on a while longer, Sergeant," Strong urged. "After we get across the Thai border, you'll be as good as home."

"Just to be out of the camp is enough," Jackson replied. "We're free. After all the years in bamboo cells and slavery, we're finally free."

"Damn right, we are," Franklin assured him. The black man offered a canteen to Jackson. "And we're never going to be in a cage again, Sarge."

"How many miles do you think we've covered so far?" Loughlin asked Muang Tzu.

"Ten or eleven kilometers," the freedom fighter answered. "How many miles is that?"

"About seven miles," Stone replied. "Seems like more than that because we've had to travel pretty slow."

"I still say I don't need to be hauled around on a stretcher," Hall insisted.

"Don't worry," Stone told him. "We're still making pretty good time. No choppers have flown overhead, so they haven't sent air patrols to search for us."

"Yeah," Gorman added as he flicked on the flame to his lighter and fired a cigarette. "If the fuckers are after us, they must be on foot."

"Put the cigarette out, Leo," Loughlin said sharply.

"We got more than a seven mile head start," Gorman replied, puffing on his cigarette. "No sweat, man."

"Unless someone radioed a Laotian army base closer to our position and they sent a squad from a different direction."

"Or waiting up ahead," Loughlin added.

"Okay," Gorman said as he dropped the cigarette and crushed it under his boot. "Sorry. I didn't think of that."

"Hey," Franklin began. "What's it like back in the States these days? I bet a lot has changed since '71. They told us a lot of crazy stuff, like Nixon was impeached and thrown out of office. Then the Ford company put one of their guys in as President."

"Yeah," Hall chuckled.

"The real funny one was they said some old movie star was elected president."

"You can read the history books and try to figure it out later," Stone replied.

"One piece of good news that you chaps will have fifteen years of back pay coming to you," Loughlin told them. "And the monthly salary for military personnel in the States has more than doubled since 1971."

"I bet the price of everything has doubled too," Hall said with a chuckle.

"Oh, yeah," Stone confirmed. "But you'll be picking up a pretty big chunk of change anyway. You fellas 'll be paid according to promotions you would have received, just from time in the service alone. Hell, Lieutenant, you're probably going to be Major Hall and Corporal Franklin is probably going to be a master sergeant."

"What about me?" Jackson asked. "Am I a sergeant major?"

"I wouldn't be surprised," Stone replied. "Anyway, you guys will have enough cash to build a new life. That's not including the bonuses paid to veterans of the Vietnam conflict. Some states even gave bonuses to military personnel who served in the armed forces during the time of the conflict, whether they actually served in 'Nam or not."

"From a P.O.W. camp to Beverly Hills," Franklin laughed. "Now that'll be a real rags-to-riches story, man."

"This all sounds great," Hall said. "But I still wonder why it took so long for anybody to come after us. Didn't they know we were being held prisoner?"

"Unconfirmed stories were floating around for years," Stone replied with a shrug. "Trying to get solid evidence about M.I.A.'s was tough. I don't know all the answers, but I agree—it was too damn long."

"You don't work for the government, do you?" Hall asked. "Those bastards were gonna let us rot, weren't they?"

Stone didn't say anything. The ex-prisoners stared down at the ground.

"Are we the last of the P.O.W.'s?" Franklin asked quietly.

"There are others," Stone said grimly. "But we'll get them out too. Later. Right now, we have to get on the road again."

"It's getting hard to see where the fuck we're going," Gorman commented. "Those dark clouds have covered up the moon."

"If it's hard for us to see," Loughlin commented. "It'll be hard for the enemy too."

"They can use flashlights," Gorman complained. "We can't."

"If they use flashlights we'll see them and . . ." the

Briton ended his sentence: the constant drone of insects had ceased.

"What is it?" Gorman asked, his voice slightly louder than a whisper.

"Shh," Stone hissed, taking his CAR from his shoulder. "There's something out there."

"Something or *someone*," Muang Tzu confirmed as he crouched by some stalks of bamboo, AK-47 in his fists.

The team fell silent. The insects did not resume their endless song. Tree frogs and night birds did not make a sound. They heard the throbbing pulse of blood behind their ears as they searched the darkness for an unknown threat.

Without warning, automatic fire erupted from the jungle. Orange flames jutted from rifle barrels among the trees and elephant grass. Stone dove into a clump of ferns as a column of bullets sizzled overhead. He heard someone moan in pain. Whoever had been hit, he managed to stifle a scream. Tough guy, whoever it was. That could have been any member of his team. They were all tough.

Stone returned fire with his CAR. He aimed at the muzzle flash of the enemies' weapons. A shriek announced he had hit a target. Stone saw Loughlin sprawled behind the trunk of a tree, firing at the enemy with his Kalashnikov rifle. Someone else opened fire as well. The weapon sounded like another AK, so it meant either a Laotian freedom fighter or one of the ex-P.O.W.'s was shooting at the unseen attackers.

"The bastards hit Jackson!" Dwayne Franklin's voice cried with anger and outrage.

More enemy fire exploded. Bullets splintered tree trunks and snapped bamboo stalks in two. Sergeant Jackson's body twisted and rolled as slugs plowed into his body. Stone clenched his teeth and cursed under his breath. After all that poor bastard had been through. After a glimmer of hope for his recovery, Jackson had been killed before he could breath air beyond the borders of Laos.

Stone fired a three round burst at the enemy and quickly rolled to a new position behind a thick log. Bullets chewed into the ferns where he had been two seconds earlier. Loughlin and the freedom fighters sprayed the attackers with lead. At least two voices screamed. One attacker fell from cover and caught several slugs in the torso before he hit the ground.

"Back up!" Stone told his men. "And watch your flanks. They outnumber us and that means they'll try to catch us in a crossfire!"

The team inched their way backward, firing at the enemy as they crawled away from the besieged position. Loughlin heard bamboo rustle from their right flank. He immediately blasted the area with Kalashnikov rounds. The outline of a man's head and shoulders appeared. Loughlin fired another burst. The attacker's head snapped back as a 7.62mm slug went through his forehead.

Dwayne Franklin saw something move in the elephant grass to their left flank. He triggered his AK-47 and slammed another opponent with a lethal dose of high velocity missiles. The muzzle flash of another weapon responded to Franklin's fire. Bullets tore into earth near the black marine's position. Lieutenant Hall aimed at the enemy gunman and blasted the aggressor with four or five rounds.

Muang Tzu and Qui Vapi sprayed twin salvos of full-auto fire at the enemy as they tried to frontal assault. Stone pulled the pin from a grenade and lobbed the M-26 blaster into the enemy's position. The grenade exploded. Two bodies were hurled into the air by the blast, Parts of them still airborne when Muang Tzu hurled a second grenade.

Brilliant light erupted from the exploding grenade. Voices shrieked. Stone noticed the remains of at least four slain opponents. All were dressed in dark clothing, some black, others dark blue, brown or green. The Laotian army had not caught up with them after all.

The attackers were bandits, Stone realized, but better

armed than most. They seemed to have a variety of
weapons. Stone recognized the familiar snarling and crack-
ing of AK-47s, but he also noticed the crisp rattle of 9mm
submachine guns, probably French MATs or British Stens.
What the hell did a bunch of bandits want with Stone's
little band? Sure, outlaws will kill a man for his shoes, but
this attack was too well coordinated, carried out by a large
number of well-armed triggermen. The effort and risk were
far greater than the potential of profit seemed to justify.

A salvo of bullets struck Qui Vapi in the back. The
Laotian guerrilla fell forward. Bullet holes between his
shoulder blades and the base of his skull told the others he
was dead. Muang Tzu and Loughlin turned toward the direction of the assassin's fire. Both men blasted the brush
with 7.62mm fury. A figure thrashed briefly in the ferns
and weeds before he fell.

Gunfire from the rear of the defenders alerted them to
another attack front. Franklin fired at the aggressors while
Hall yanked the pin from a grenade and hurled it at the
enemy. Another explosion ripped two or three opponents
apart. Abruptly the shooting stopped.

"Pi-wye-wye!" a voice shouted. *"Pi-wye-wye!"*

The commander was recalling his troops to revise his
strategy, but Stone suspected the guy was too smart to call
all his troops back to one position unless he planned to
retreat. He only hoped that the attackers planned to pull
out. Bandits are not accustomed to fighting opponents who
cost them such high numbers of casualties.

"How's everybody doing?" Stone called out.

"Two dead," Loughlin replied. "Maybe three. I don't
know what happened to Leo."

"Damn," Stone rasped. "Is everybody else still in one
piece?"

"As far as I can tell," the Brit answered.

"Our opponents are not soldiers," Muang Tzu announced.

"Yeah," Stone replied. "I noticed that too."

"What the fuck are they attackin' us for?" Franklin

wondered aloud. "They need some C-rations or something?"

"Probably figured they'd hit a small group and take whatever they found," Hall answered. "They'll back off now. We must have killed a dozen of them. Bandits are practical. They'll haul ass and try to find victims who don't fight back like we do."

"I wouldn't count on that," Loughlin remarked. "They don't seem to be the sort that discourage easily."

"I think that's because we have something they want," Stone stated. "Notice they didn't throw any grenades at us? They could probably have wiped us out pretty easy if they did."

"Maybe they don't have any," Franklin suggested.

"They seem to have everything else," Loughlin answered. "Not that difficult to make your own grenades if you have to."

"True," Muang Tzu agreed. "So what do they want, Mark?"

"They want us alive or at least in recognizable condition," Stone explained. "Somehow they must have found out about the prison break. The bandits are playing bounty hunter. They must figure the Laotian army will pay for us . . . dead or alive."

"But they won't pay for a few buckets of human parts," Loughlin added. "Which is all they'd have if they hit us with grenades."

"Maybe we should pull a dirty trick on them and blow ourselves up," Franklin commented. "I think I'd rather do that than be taken captive again."

"Quiet!" Stone said sharply.

He heard faint rustling among the bamboo and leaves. The sound was everywhere. The enemy was moving closer, but they were holding their fire. Stone's group did likewise. Their ammo was getting low and they could not afford to use up rounds unless they were relatively certain they could hit a target. Bushes parted near Muang Tzu and a shape poked through. The Laotian nearly opened fire, but he recognized Leo Gorman in time to move his finger from the trigger.

"Shit, Leo," Loughlin complained. "You want to get yourself shot? We've got enough trouble without killing each other."

"Oh, yeah?" Gorman replied with a grin as he waved his Uzi.

"Please, be more careful," Muang Tzu sighed as he turned his back to Gorman.

"Sure, gook," the mercenary mused as he pointed the barrel of his subgun at the back of Muang Tzu's skull and squeezed the trigger.

The Laotian freedom fighter's head exploded. Nearly decapitated, Muang Tzu's corpse dropped to the ground. Stone and Loughlin turned sharply to see the muzzle of Gorman's Uzi aimed at them.

"Drop your guns," Gorman ordered. "No tricks."

"Son of a bitch," Loughlin whispered.

"If you're still alive you can talk a deal," Gorman suggested. "Khong Noh loves deals. Drop the guns."

"Khong Noh," Stone commented. "So you two are on a first name basis. You planned to sell us out from the start."

"It was you they were gunning for in Bangkok," Loughlin said as he slowly stepped away from Stone. "You made some sort of deal with them, to get yourself off the hook."

"One more step and you're both dead," Gorman warned. "Last time. Drop the fuckin' guns."

Stone reluctantly dropped his CAR-15 and Loughlin released his AK-47. Both men still carried pistols. If one could draw Gorman's attention, the other might be able to take him out. Stone raised his hands to shoulder level. Since he carried his Beretta in a shoulder holster, he had a better chance of drawing his weapon with his hands raised. Loughlin was aware of this and placed both hands on the top of his head, far from the .45 Colt on his hip.

"What about Hall and Franklin?" Stone asked. "Are they part of the deal?"

"Shut up," Gorman replied simply.

"You make Judas look like a saint, Gorman," Loughlin remarked, slowly moving his fingers from his his head as if preparing to lower his hands.

"Hold it!" Gorman warned, aiming his Uzi at the Briton's chest.

Stone's right hand plunged to the pistol grips of his Beretta. Suddenly, a hard metal cylinder jabbed the small of his back. Stone froze, aware the object at his spine was a gun barrel.

"Don't be foolish," Khong Noh warned. His English was flawless, with a slight Cambridge accent. "The battle is lost. To resist would mean death for all five of you."

Stone noticed Hall and Franklin were seated on the ground with their hands held over head. Two bandits held guns aimed at the ex-P.O.W.'s chests and three other enemy gunmen stood behind the Americans with weapons pointed at their backs.

Khong Noh and several of his men approached Stone. He recognized Khong Noh as the leader of the bandits. The tall, athletically slender Khong Noh moved with a confident stride, his posture ramrod straight, his head held high.

"Which one of you is Mark Stone?" Khong Noh demanded.

"I am," Stone replied. "Gorman must have gotten quite a bit of information to you."

"Not that much," the bandit leader smiled. "Allow me to introduce myself. I am Khong Noh, commander of an enforcement section of a major business enterprise system of Southeast Asia."

"Opium," Stone remarked.

"Of course," Khong Noh said with a shrug. "You Americans are familiar with the free enterprise system. Goods and services. Supply and demand. My friends in the Communist government will deny this, of course, but one way or the other, supply and demand applies everywhere in the world. As long as people want opium and they're willing to pay for it, someone will be willing to sell it to them. I supply my own humble services of protection for these narcotics salesmen."

"That's cute, Khong Noh," Stone said dryly. "You make yourself sound like you're more than just a thug who sells dope and gives other thugs orders to break legs and kill people."

"Oh, I'm more than that," Khong Noh replied. "I assure you, Mister Stone. You're a rather colorful and exceptional man as well. Why, you've become something of a legend. The brave American veteran who rescues his fellow countrymen from the clutches of Communist P.O.W. camps. How melodramatic."

Without warning, Khong Noh's fist shot out. It was a short punch, but he struck with the big knuckles of the first and second fingers, in the manner of a karate or kung fu punch. The blow caught Stone on the tip of the chin hard enough to knock him on his ass.

"You and your friends killed fifteen of my men, Mister Stone," Khong Noh hissed. "You all shall pay for that. But you will pay the most . . . because you are their leader. The price of leadership can be very high."

"Yeah," Stone replied as he rubbed his sore jaw. "You might remember that can apply to you too."

"How droll," Khong Noh smiled. "Of course, I won't kill you, Mister Stone. But, before we're finished with you, you might wish we had."

Chapter Fifteen

Khong Noh's men disarmed Stone, Loughlin, and the former P.O.W.'s. They frisked the Americans thoroughly, taking every firearm, knife, garrote and cartridge. The bandits handcuffed their prisoners, locking their wrists together at the small of each man's back. Nick Hall and Dwayne Franklin were especially upset by this. They trembled, not from fear as much as the terrible disappointment that freedom had been so short-lived.

Gorman tried to avoid looking at the prisoners. He strolled over to Khong Noh and Ban Xiang. The bandit chief and his second in command smiled at the merc. Gorman forced a weak grin in return.

"Well, I kept my word," the merc declared. "You've got Mark Stone and the P.O.W.'s, just as I promised."

"Yes," Khong Noh said with a nod. "I must admit, I never would have thought you'd do anything quite this daring, Leo."

"I figured I had to come up with something pretty good in order to convince you to wipe the slate clean after that little mistake I made."

"Then you admit you stole the thirty kilos of opium?"

Khong Noh remarked. "We had a talk with Thay Komgi just yesterday. He claimed it was all your fault. He said you made him go along with the theft."

"You didn't believe him, did you?" Gorman asked. "I mean, it was his idea—"

"Well, he can neither admit to that or deny it," Khong Noh said with a shrug. "You see, Thay Komgi is no longer with us. He died shortly after our discussion."

"Yeah?" Gorman trembled slightly. He gripped the frame of his Uzi and slid his fingers toward the trigger. "Well, good riddance. Fucker was a troublemaker. Didn't even try to square things with you like I did."

"Actually, you caused me quite a bit of trouble, Leo," Khong Noh declared. "The opium suppliers were upset because they lost merchandise and a considerable profit. The government was unhappy because you killed three soldiers before you fled to Thailand. Naturally, they were upset with me. I lost face because of you, Leo. You've spent a fair amount of time in the Orient, but I don't think you ever understood what it means to us to lose face. It means a man's honor has become questionable. It means he must prove his honesty, integrity, and courage."

"I lost face with you," Gorman said. "But I've tried to regain it. I kept my word and you said yourself it took guts. We're going to make a hell of a profit on these guys, Khong Noh."

"Enough to compensate for the spiritual torment you caused me?" the bandit leader sighed. "That would be quite a feat, Leo."

"Look," Gorman began, sweating with fear as he realized the deal might not save him after all. "How about I just give these guys to you. Stone and his buddy, the P.O.W.'s and . . . and you keep all the profit when you sell 'em to the government. Okay?"

"You'll give them to me?" Khong Noh laughed. "But I've already got them now."

"Just call off your dogs, man," Gorman said. "That's all I ask."

"Agreed," Khong Noh assured him. "I will send no more hired assassins to hunt you down and kill you. Is that what you want, Leo?"

"Yeah," the mercenary nearly fainted with relief. "That's what I want. Thank you, Khong Noh."

"You're welcome, Leo," the bandit leader said. "Now, you realize, I must not lose face again."

"I'll never do anything to cause you trouble in the future," Gorman promised. "I swear to God, Khong Noh."

"I'm not referring to that," Khong Noh replied. "You see, I promised something to Ban Xiang."

Gorman turned toward the bandit's second in command. Ban Xiang pointed a Walther P-38 at the mercenary's face. The bandit lieutenant smiled at the terror in Gorman's bulging eyes.

"I gave him my word he could kill you," Khong Noh explained with a smile.

Leo Gorman desperately reached for his Uzi. His grip had relaxed when he thought he had been forgiven. Ben Xiang fired his Walther pistol. A nine millimeter bullet smashed between Gorman's eyes, split his skull and drilled into his brain. Leo Gorman's corpse fell. Ban Xiang spat on the body.

"That settles our business with Leo Gorman," Khong Noh announced as he turned toward the other prisoners. "I don't imagine the execution of that traitor causes any grief for you gentlemen. He betrayed me and he betrayed you. Such a corrupt individual could never be trusted. We're all better off without Leo Gorman."

"I'm not going to cry," Stone replied. "But I don't feel like cheering either. What happens now, Khong Noh?"

"Now you get to rest," the bandit chief replied. "We've all had a long day and we can do with some sleep before we start moving out. Sleeping with your hands chained isn't terribly comfortable, but necessary, for reasons which should be obvious to you all. Naturally, guards will be posted to make certain none of you sleepwalk and injure yourselves. We mustn't have that. No harm is to come to you gentlemen until it can be administered scientifically."

"Isn't torture a little crude for a refined gentleman like you?" Stone sneered.

"Crude, but effective," Khong Noh said. "I've already told you that you must be punished. Besides, I need some information from you. Details about your previous assaults on other P.O.W. camps. Locations, names, tactics used, that sort of thing. We also want to know about the other group which was with you after the raid in the plateau region."

"What other group?" Stone asked with a blank expression.

"Don't lie about something we already know, Mister Stone," Khong Noh warned. "We've been watching you through infrared telescopes since you attacked the camp. A group of twelve Asians, most of them former P.O.W.'s, headed south while your group moved west, toward the Thai border. Since there were no Caucasians in that group, we let them go. We wanted you and the American P.O.W.'s—you're far more valuable than a few native rebels, trying to fight the Communists."

"But you want to know about them anyway," Loughlin remarked.

"I don't," Khong Noh assured him. "But the government will certainly want to know about them."

"Lieutenant Hall and Corporal Franklin aren't in very good physical condition after being P.O.W.'s for fifteen years," Stone told the bandit leader. "If you torture them, there's a pretty good chance you'll kill them in the process."

"Don't worry about them," Khong Noh replied. "I have no intention of losing such valuable merchandise because a heart could not stand the strain of torture. You see, I am experienced in these matters, Mister Stone."

"That's not the best bloody news we've heard all week," Loughlin muttered.

"You're English, aren't you?" Khong Noh remarked. "I learned English from a British tutor. I believe he was some sort of missionary. Must have been more than twenty years ago. Stupid fellow thought that Christianity could somehow save the world. I've always wondered if all Britons are as stupid as that one. It will be interesting to see what I can learn from you."

"Plenty of new profanity," Loughlin replied simply. "Not much else."

"I'd better get more than that," Khong Noh warned. "You're not as valuable to me as Stone and the P.O.W.'s, my British friend. You'd do well to cooperate, if you want to stay alive."

Loughlin opened his mouth to make a crude remark, but decided it would be foolish under the circumstances. Khong Noh snapped orders to his men. The bandits shoved their captives into a group and forced them to sit beneath a tree. Rope was wound around their chests to bind them to the trunk. Sentries stood guard by the prisoners while the rest of the bandits set up camp for the night.

"Oh, sweet Jesus," Franklin sobbed. Being a prisoner again was simply too much to bear. After his prayers had finally been answered, his hopes had been dashed once more.

A guard stepped toward Franklin and lashed out a boot. He He kicked the black marine in the face. Franklin's head snapped to the side. blood oozed from the corner of his mouth, and a bruise appeared on his left cheek.

"*Bau tiang!*" the guard barked, addressing his order of "no talk" to all four prisoners.

Stone closed his eyes and breathed deeply, trying to relax his muscles to ease tensions. There was nothing they could do for now. Perhaps a better opportunity would come along later, but until then all they could do was try to rest —and pray for a miracle.

Hog Wiley scratched his shaggy beard as he impatiently waited outside the Buddhist shrine. Several Asians sat on the stone steps of the pagoda-style temple. Hog glanced up at the building and watched two men with shaven heads, dressed in orange robes reverently walk past a row of gilded Buddhas.

"You boys sure about this Viang Tha character?" Wiley asked his companions. "I kinda wonder about a fightin' man who spends his free time in a shrine prayin' instead of gettin' drunk and gettin' laid."

"Viang Tha is a deeply religious man," Lan Nhung, a Laotian freedom fighter replied. "It was his religious convictions which turned him against the Communists and their athiest philosophy. Communists persecute Buddhists and Taoists, as well as Christians and Jews, you know."

"Yeah," Hog said, glancing at his wrist watch. "But I wanna get the fuck outta here. This is supposed to be a goddamn mission, not a prayer meetin'."

"I'm with you, Jack," Tak Chao agreed. He was a Thai soldier of fortune who had learned most of his English from American mercs on missions into Cambodia during the mid-1970s. "We're spinning wheels when we should be shooting the shit from Commie assholes."

"Yet, we must respect the religious devotion of Viang Tha," Thani Son Chiang remarked. He was also a Thai mercenary, but far more soft-spoken and polite than Tak Chao. "After all, most young men in Thailand spend a year or two in a monastery."

"We sure as shit ain't gonna wait a fuckin' year for Viang Tha," Hog growled. "As a matter of fact, that guy's got five minutes. If he's not out here by then, fuck it. We're goin' without him."

"Here he comes, Mister Wiley," Lan Nhung announced.

"Shit, boy," Wiley commented. "I ain't your daddy. Just call me Hog. Everytime somebody calls me 'Mister Wiley!' I start lookin' around to see if one of my relatives walked in. You call me 'Mister Wiley' in a firefight, you might distract me so bad I might get a bullet up my ass before I know you was just fuckin' around with my name again."

"Sorry, Mister Hog," the Laotian replied.

"That's better," Wiley said with a nod.

Viang Tha descended the stairs. His height was average for a Laotian, roughly five-and-a-half feet tall. He was slender, with a lean face and long, jet black hair, combed back from his high forehead. A black patch covered his left eye. He had lost it four years earlier in a battle with the Communists near the Meong delta.

"Howdy," Hog greeted. "I was told you speak English real good, Viang Tha. Glad to hear it 'cause my Lao sucks worse than a cheap whore with buck teeth."

"Pouak-chao men-pi?" Viang Tha demanded. He addressed the question to Hog, but his hard gaze turned toward Lan Nhung.

"Just call me Hog," Wiley replied. "Don't give Lan Nhung no dirty looks. At lest I found him where he was supposed to be, fuckin' away in a whorehouse. And speak English. Okay?"

"Okay," Viang Tha said with a slow nod. "What do you want, Pig?"

"Hog, fella," Wiey bellowed. "Get it right and keep it right. Last man who called me a pig is probably still wearin' his asshole for a collar. What I want is a little business deal."

"I am listening, Hog," Viang Tha assured him.

"You fellas want weapons and ammunition to fight the Reds," Wiley began. "But you're a bit short on cash. Now, my buddy An Khom would be happier than a pig in shit to give you what you need and not charge you a plugged penny for it. What would that be? About a third of a kip. Anyway, An Khom would like to just give you the fuckin' guns and ammo, but he's gotta make a livin' just like the rest of us. Now, 'cause he's a good pal of mine, I can get weapons wholesale. Get you lots of stuff for blowin' people up and blastin' holes in 'em."

"But you want a favor?" Viang Tha said suspiciously.

"You got it, old boy," Hog confirmed.

"We do not deal in opium or any other sort of drug traffic," the Laotian said grimly, his hand sliding inside his jacket.

"Shit," Wiley snorted. "I didn't say a thing about any fuckin' dope. So just keep your piece in it's holster, Viang Tha. That ain't the kinda deal I'm interested in."

"Then I'm still listening," the Laotian replied.

"Some friends of mine are already in Laos on a mission to rescue a bunch of P.O.W.'s from a prison camp in the *Plateau des* region," Hog explained. "Now, there's a fella with them who might be a desperato. You know, a crooked cocksucker mixed up with opium traffic and hill bandits. From the way you were talkin' before, I reckon you don't have much use for those scumbags and neither do I. Trouble is, this little fucker might set my buddies up. They don't know what a no-good hoot owl they've got with 'em."

"So you'll give us the weapons and ammunition—if we help you find your friends," Viang Tha said. "Is that what you propose?"

The hulking Texan flashed a crooked grin. "Hit the nail right on the head, buddy boy," he replied.

Chapter Sixteen

The first rays of daybreak woke Mark Stone. Glancing about he was surprised to discover there was no guard stationed near the four prisoners. Two sentries were near the edge of the camp, and another man was relieving himself against the base of a tree trunk. At least this guard had the decency not to piss on the captives. The strong scent of urine assaulted Stone's nostrils and explained the damp spot on his pant leg.

"Loughlin?" Stone whispered.

"I'm awake," the Briton replied. "You have any brilliant ideas about how we're going to get out of this?"

"We go with the best opportunity we get," Stone replied.

"You think we can uproot this fuckin' tree?" Dwayne Franklin's voice rasped bitterly. "Or break our cuffs? I ain't been eating my spinach lately. It wasn't part of the diet."

"Maybe they'll untie us," Hall added. "But I don't think they'll take the cuffs off."

"They might if they feed us," Stone declared.

"Feed us?" Franklin scoffed. "Dream on, man. These

137

are bandits. You think they give a shit about our growling stomachs?"

"I'm afraid Dwayne's right," Hall added. "The goddamn Laotian army barely kept us alive. I hate to think how these bastards are gonna treat us."

"They want us alive and fairly healthy," Stone stated. He whispered rapidly, noticing that the guard by the tree was buttoning his trousers. "They won't shoot us unless they figure that's the only way to stop us. They won't shoot to kill unless they absolutely have to. Khong Noh isn't stupid. He knows American P.O.W.'s are used for propaganda in Laos. You're more valuable alive than dead. He figures he can get money for me too, so he won't want to do anything that'll risk killing me."

"Guess I'm shit out of luck," Loughlin muttered sourly. "Mister Waterfall is headed this way."

Loughlin referred to the guard who had relieved himself at the tree. The bandit strolled back to the prisoners. He glanced down at them and noticed they were awake. He removed a canteen from his belt, opened the top and held the mouth of the bottle to Stone's lips. The American vet half expected the canteen to be filled with urine, but the water tasted fine. Stone drank thankfully.

"Xin cam on ong lam lam," Stone said, thanking him in Vietnamese because he was not certain how to say it in Lao.

"You're welcome," the guard replied in English.

"You're full of surprises," Stone remarked. "Sure you won't get in trouble for giving us water?"

"No," the guard assured him as he offered the canteen to Loughlin. "Khong Noh didn't order us to mistreat you or let you go thirsty. If he had wanted that, he would have told us. He's not a bad leader. That's hard for you to believe, I'm sure, but Khong Noh looks after his people. I'm just supposed to keep you men from escaping and there's no reason to abuse you in the meantime."

"Your attitude is a bit different than the bloke who

guarded us earlier," Loughlin stated. "He kicked Franklin in the face for praying out loud."

"He's angry with you," the guard replied in English as he held the canteen for Hall. "You killed fifteen of our men last night. We're pretty close to each other in this band. The men you killed are like brothers to us. We grieve for them."

"How come you're treating us in such a civilized manner," Hall wanted to know.

"You killed some good friends of mine," the guard began, giving water to Franklin. "But you were acting in self-defense. I don't blame you for that. I would have done the same. Unfortunately for you, most of the others don't share my view."

"I know this is a silly question," Loughlin began. "But, would you consider helping us to escape?"

"I'm afraid not," the guard chuckled as he poured some water over the bruise on Franklin's face. "These people are my family. I can't betray them."

"You don't seem much like a bandit," Stone remarked. "Maybe you should find a new family. One with principles more like your own."

"Oh?" the guard raised his eyebrows. "Do you suggest I become a rebel and fight the Communists like your Laotian allies? I used to be a so-called freedom fighter. I was part of a band which intended to overthrow the Communists and establish a republic. Other groups are trying to set up a socialist system. There's even a group of freedom fighters who intend to put a fellow who claims to be related to the late King Sisavang Vong in power and establish a new monarchy."

"I know the freedom fighters need to be more organized," Stone replied. "Maybe you're the man to unite them so they can succeed in overthrowing the Communists once and for all."

"I'm the man, eh?" the guard laughed. "No. That's romantic nonsense. The Communists are too powerful.

They're backed by Vietnam and the Soviets. It's impossible to overthrow a Communist government."

"If you believe that," Stone sighed. "I feel sorry for you."

"Feel sorry for yourself," the guard replied. "You're going to merit pity more than I."

"I haven't compromised myself because the odds got tough," Stone told him. "What's your name?"

"That hardly matters," the guard answered. "I doubt we'll get a chance to talk again anyway."

"Well, thanks for the water anyway," Stone said with a shrug.

"I see our guests are awake," Khong Noh announced, as he rose from his bedroll and slowly stretched his arms overhead. "Ready to face the new day's events?"

"I've got a question, Khong Noh," Stone began. "How much money do you plan to make by selling us to the Laotian government?"

"I plan to get a million kip for you alone, Mister Stone," the bandit leader stated. He tilted his head to breath deeply through his nose. He lowered his chin and exhaled. "Each P.O.W. will probably be worth about half that. I don't know about the Englishman yet."

"How about three million baht for the lot of us?" Stone inquired. "That would be about three and a half million kip, right?"

"Close enough," Khong Noh smiled. "The baht is Thai currency. I take it you're offering to pay your own ransom."

"Friends of mine will pay it," Stone answered. "I'll tell you how to contact them and we'll arrange an exchange. Three million baht for the four of us."

"An interesting proposal," the bandit leader admitted. He strapped on his gun belt. Khong Noh carried only one weapon. It was a Soviet-made Stechkin machinepistol. "Who would be paying for this? The American C.I.A.?"

"Do you care?" Stone replied. "As long as you get the money, what difference does it make?"

"Good point," Khong Noh agreed. He smelled the aroma of freshly brewed tea and boiled rice with vegetables and water buffalo strips. "Breakfast is ready. Let's discuss business over a good morning meal."

Bowls of food and tea cups were prepared and placed on a low table. Khong Noh and Ban Xiang sat cross-legged at the table and waited for Stone. The ropes were removed and the four prisoners were permitted to rise. They groaned as blood began to flow painfully into their stiffened limbs. A bandit unlocked Stone's handcuffs.

"What about my friends?" Stone asked Khong Noh. "Don't they get to eat?"

"Not at the business table," the bandit leader replied. "But they'll be fed . . . and closely guarded in case this is some sort of idiot trick, Mister Stone."

"Can I talk to them for a second?"

"No," Khong Noh replied simply.

"Go on, Stone," Lieutenant Nick Hall whispered. "If you can make a deal with the Devil, do it. If not, the rest of you try to escape. I'll hold 'em off as long as I can."

"We're all getting out," Loughin rasped.

"I can't run with a crippled leg," Hall replied. "You'd never make it tryin' to carry me. Better that three escape, then we all go down together."

A burly guard grabbed Stone and shoved him toward the table. The bandit turned sharply and swatted the back of his hand across Hall's face. Stone balled his fists, but did not raise them. He was surrounded by armed opponents. It would be ridiculous to start a fight with the brutal Laotian under such circumstances.

"Mister Stone," Khong Noh gestured at the table. "I'm getting impatient."

Stone sat at the table and bowed to his host. Khong Noh returned the gesture. Ban Xiang pushed a bowl of rice with meat and vegetables toward Stone. No chopsticks were given to him.

"I have to eat with my fingers?" Stone inquired.

"We can't afford to be careless with you," Khong Noh

said. "I don't think you're foolish enough to try to lunge at
me with a chopstick and attempt to stab it through my
throat or eyesocket. But let's avoid the temptation."

"Well, don't complain about my table manners," Stone
commented. Ban Xiang offered him a damp cloth to wash
his hands. "You fellows don't believe in taking chances."

"No more than we can avoid," Khong Noh confirmed.
"Now, let's hear you're business proposal, Mister Stone."

"Okay. You need to contact a C.I.A. case officer located
at the outskirts of Bangkok. Tell him I've been jeopar-
dized. Either the Company pays for my release, or the
Communists will get me."

"I see," Khong Noh mused. "What's this man's name?"

"Kirkmeyer," Stone lied. He had no reason to like Alan
Coleman, but he didn't want to burn the C.I.A. man's
cover any worse than Coleman and his agents had done
already. "Samuel Kirkmeyer."

"The address?" the bandit leader asked.

Stone gave him the address of a radio repair shop which
he knew to be a K.G.B. front for Soviet intelligence gath-
ering operations in Bangkok. If Khong Noh actually tried
to follow Stone's lead, the bandit would find himself in a
very confusing and potentially dangerous situation.

"And you think this Kirkmeyer will pay three million
baht for you and your three friends?" Khong Noh inquired.

"You might haggle," Stone suggested. "Try for five
million. He'll say two and a half. Try for four and he'll say
three. You might be able to get him up to three and a half
million, but I doubt it. He doesn't like me much, but he
knows I'm valuable."

"How would this payment be made?" Khong Noh
asked. "I don't take checks, money orders or savings
bonds, you know."

"Of course not," Stone said as he chewed a mouthful of
rice and vegetables. "Payment can be made in Thai baht,
American dollars, or commodities."

"Commodities?" Khong Noh raised his eyebrows.
"Gold, silver or diamonds?"

"Gold or diamonds, or a combination of the two," Stone answered. "The diamonds would be small, uncut stones. Impossible to trace. The gold would probably be imported form India in standard *tolas*. That's a unit of measurement, about half an ounce."

"Intriguing," the bandit smiled. "What if the C.I.A. only wants you, and they're not interested in the P.O.W.'s."

"What do you think they hire me for?" Stone replied with a shrug. "My job is to recover American M.I.A.'s anywhere I find them. You don't think I do this as a hobby, do you?"

"I'm not quite certain why you do anything, Mister Stone," Khong Noh stated. "And I suspect you're playing for a time, as you Americans say. Is that expression still popular in your country?"

"It doesn't apply in this case, Khong Noh," Stone assured him. "I'm telling you the truth."

"So you expect us to simply detain you and the others while I contact my sources in Bangkok and have them check this information?" Khong Noh laughed. "The problem with that idea is the fact the Laotian army has probably learned what has happened to the P.O.W. camp by now. They're probably searching for you and your companions even as we speak. That means I don't have a great deal of time, Mister Stone."

"But you had planned to sell me to the C.I.A. if they offered you a better deal than the Communists," Stone reminded him. "And the Company will pay more, Khong Noh. You know that as well as I do."

"I know no such thing," the bandit replied. "However, I had planned to contact the C.I.A. via the American Embassy in Bangkok. Every country shuffles intelligence agents through embassies, although they all claim they don't. I can be fairly certain of contacting the C.I.A. in this manner, but if I follow your instructions, I might simply waste time chasing a wild duck, as you might say."

"You mean a wild goose chase," Stone commented. "No problem, Khong Noh. Why don't you try to contact the

C.I.A. through the embassy and check with Kirkmeyer at the same time. The Company will pay off a lot faster. If you try to contact the then via the embassy, they'll spend a week denying they even exist and another week of fooling around with red tape and counterintelligence crap. They'll still be arguing with accountants while Kirkmeyer is arranging the exchange."

"You sound convincing, Mister Stone," Khong Noh commented.

"You can always check my story and judge for yourself," Stone suggested as he sipped tea.

"I intend to," the bandit leader assured him. "Now. . ."

Shouts of alarm startled the bandits. Stone glanced over his shoulder to see Loughlin, Franklin, and Hall no longer wearing handcuffs. The bandits had served the prisoners breakfast while three armed guards watched the trio. Lieutenant Hall had made the first move in a desperate bid for freedom. The marine officer had leaped forward with his one good leg and dove into two guards, shoving their weapons toward the ground. All three men hit the dirt in a struggling heap.

Loughlin had quickly taken advantage of this distraction. He slapped the barrel of an AK-47 out of the grasp of the third guard, and deflected the aim of the weapon. The Briton slashed a karate chop to his opponent's windpipe, and yanked the rifle from the bandit's hands. The guard staggered and fell dying, both hands clasped to his crushed throat.

"Party's over," Stone growled as he tossed his tea into Khong Noh's face.

The bandit leader shouted something in Lao and pawed at his eyes. Ban Xiang started to rise and reached for the Walther P-38 on his hip. Stone hurled the teacup at the bandit lieutenant's head. Ban Xiang instinctively ducked and the cup bounced off his shoulder.

The distraction bought Stone a second or two. Long enough to jump to his feet and attack the closest guard. He recognized the face of the bandit who had given them water when the prisoners were tied to the tree. The man no longer seemed friendly as he swung a French MAT subma- chine gun at the ex-Green Beret.

Stone threw a round-house kick which sent the subgun flying from the bandit's grasp. He snapped a backfist to the guard's face and dove for the fallen MAT. Two pistol shots snarled. Stone heard someone groan. He hit the ground near the subgun, scooped up the weapon and rolled to one knee.

The bandit who had tried to stop Stone stared down at him. Blood flowed from the man's broken nose. Other crimson stains spread from twin bulletholes in his chest. A weak smile played at the guard's lips before he fell dead.

Stone swung the French blaster toward Khong Noh and Ban Xiang. The bandit lieutenant held his Walther in both hands. A curl of smoke from the muzzle revealed that Ban Xiang's weapon had killed the guard. Stone opened fire.

Three 9mm parabellum rounds chopped into Ban Xiang's chest. The impact lifted him off his feet and hurled him into the air. The second in command of Khong Noh's band crashed to earth in a bloodied lump, while the bandit chief ducked for cover behind the trunk of a tree.

Dwayne Franklin kicked a Laotian outlaw in the groin and knocked him down with a solid right cross. The black marine dropped on the fallen bandit, his knee landing on the man's diaphragm with all his weight behind it. The bandit gasped in stunned agony as Franklin wrenched an AK-47 from his fingers. He stamped the butt into the guard's forehead and crushed the Laotian's skull.

A bandit clubbed Lieutenant Hall from behind with the butt of his rifle, and the marine officer sprawled senseless at the Laotian's feet. Loughlin spun and raised his Kalash- nikov and fired three rounds into the torso of the bandit. The outlaw screamed and fell.

Two bandits pointed their weapons at the former S.A.S. commando, but Stone's MAT-49 submachine gun sprayed the pair before they could trigger a single shot. Nine milli- meter slugs ripped into the outlaws and sent them tumbling back into another group of would-be opponents. The startled reinforcements were splattered with the blood of slain comrades. They dove to the ground, more concerned with self-preservation than stopping the escaping prisoners.

Loughlin dashed for the edge of the camp, running for the cover of the jungle. A column of bullets slashed air above his head. The Briton fell to one knee and pivoted his AK at an enemy gunman with a British-made Sten.

The S.A.S. trained pro blasted a trio of 7.62mm slugs into the stomach and chest of his attacker. The bandit dropped his submachinegun and crumbled to the ground, as Khong Noh fired his Stechkin from the cover of a tree. Nine millimeters tore dirt from the ground near Loughlin's feet. The Briton dove for a clump of ferns.

Stone fired a quick volley at Khong Noh's position. Bullets chipped bark from the tree, and forced the bandit leader to stay behind his cover. Stone raced for the edge of the woods.

Franklin fired his Kalashnikov from the hip. Bullets smashed the chest and face of an approaching bandit. Another dead outlaw collapsed, and Dwayne Franklin dashed into the cover of the bamboo and trees.

A violent explosion erupted from the jungle. Franklin's body was hurled back into the open. He hit the ground and rolled twice. Dozens of small wounds leaked crimson. The marine moaned as he tried to rise. Then he passed out. His rifle dropped onto ground beside him.

The explosion also knocked Loughlin to the ground. Stone could not see if his British friend was seriously wounded or not, but he saw three bandits charge toward Loughlin's position. Stone fired into the trio. One bandit fell and the others dove to the ground.

Stone's MAT clicked when he squeezed the trigger. The weapon was empty. Khong Noh and two other bandits quickly approached, weapons held ready.

"You have no ammunition left, Stone," Khong Noh announced, his voice cold and hard. The bandit leader no longer seemed concerned with social pleasantries. His expression revealed pure hatred. "If you try to run into the jungle, you might trigger a trip wire and set off one of the booby traps we set beyond the camp."

"Looks like you guys win round two," Stone admitted, tossing down his French subgun and raising his hands in surrender.

"And you lose," Khong Noh declared as he stepped closer and pointed the Stechkin pistol at Stone's face. "You lose everything, Stone."

The bandit leader's foot shot out and caught Stone between the legs. White hot agony sizzled from his genitals, branching through his nervous system. Stone gasped and started to double up. Khong Noh backhanded the barrel of his Russian machinepistol across the American's face. Stone fell, his head ringing with pain.

A kick to his stomach forced his body to jackknife on the ground. Fingers clawed into his hair and jerked his head forward. Stone's vision was blurred, but he saw the outline of a man's shape and the fist which rocketed toward his face. Rock hard knuckles crashed into Stone's jaw. It was the last thing he saw before he plunged into a black pit of unconsciousness.

Chapter Seventeen

Hog Wiley and his band of freedom fighters and mercenaries had slipped across the border into Laos just before dawn. Dressed in camouflage uniforms, the strike force had slithered under barbed wire and crawled through elephant grass for more than an hour, keeping low to avoid the Laotian military patrols. Wiley located a group of boulders and crawled to it. His Laotian and Thai companions followed.

"Reckon everybody's knees and elbows feel like shit by now," the burly Texan remarked. "Let's get up and rest a spell."

"A spell?" Lan Nhung was confused by the expression. The Laotian was familiar with the word "spell" in regard to writing words. Hog's use seemed of the term seemed absurd to the freedom fighter.

"Rest for a while," Wiley explained. He sat up and leaned his back against a boulder. "No smokin' and no talkin' a whisper. Could be soldiers creepin' around near by. Can't be too fuckin' careful when you're doin' this sorta shit."

"It's chilly, dude," Tak Chao replied with an idiot grin. Some of the strike force were inclined to think there was a good reason for this.

"Chilly?" Lan Nhung wondered aloud. "but it is very hot today..."

"Don't pay any attention to anything Tak Chao says in English," Thani Son Chiang urged. "It never makes any sense."

"Blow it out your ears, jack," the other Thai merc replied.

"This is no time for petty quarrels," Viang Tha hissed. "All right, Hog, we're across the border. Now what?"

"You tell me," Wiley replied. "This is your country. You used to be a paratrooper in the Laotian army. They got any army bases around here?"

"There's an air base ten kilometers east," Viang Tha answered. "Fourteen kilometers to the north, you'll find an infantry base. Of course, there are smaller units along the border. We slipped past them without any problem, but don't forget about patrols. The Communists are worried about enemies slipping into Laos from Thailand, but they're equally concerned about Laotians trying to flee the country. More than two hundred thousand Laotians fled after the Communists took over in 1975."

"An Khom mentioned that you used to be a helicopter pilot, Viang Tha," Wiley mused. "Is that right?"

"Yes," the Laotian confirmed. "But I don't see how that matters. We don't have a helicopter..."

"Not yet," the Texan said with a grin.

"You can't be thinking what I'm afraid you're thinking," Viang Tha groaned. "You've said more than three sentences without profanity, Hog. Maybe that's restricting your ability to think in a rational manner."

"Shit no," Hog assured him. "I'm not crazy, Viang Tha. If we can get to that air base and steal a chopper, then we can comb the plateaus and surrounding area for my buddies and the fellas with 'em. That'd save a hell of a lot of time."

"That's what I was afraid you were going to say," Viang Tha sighed. "Forget it, Hog. Better come up with another plan."

"We're runnin' out of time," Wiley insisted. "My partners are shovelin' shit against a tidal wave and I ain't gonna stand around beatin' my meat while they go under."

"The profanity doesn't seem to be helping," Thani Son Chiang commented. "Listen, Hog, there are only eight of us. That's not enough manpower to take on an air base. We'd never get close to a helicopter. The enemy would cut us to ribbons before we could get inside the base, let alone steal an aircraft."

"You can't say anything's impossible until you've checked out the situation," Hog declared. "Maybe it won't be as hard as you reckon it'll be."

"Even if we could steal a helicoptor," Viang Tha added. "And mind you, I said 'if' and 'could', it wouldn't take them long to find us. They'd send other aircraft after us, or shoot us out of the sky with antiaircraft weapons. Have you ever heard of radar?"

"Sure," Wiley said with a nod. "Looks sorta like a TV."

"I hope you aren't serious about this," Viang Tha commented.

"Wait a fuckin' minute," Hog said sharply. "How many trackin' stations do they have this far south? The Russkies supplied this country with most of the technical shit, right? Did they just hand over plenty of extra gear and tell the natives to try to cover every fuckin' inch of air space?"

"Hardly," Viang Tha admitted.

"Damn right they didn't," Wiley agreed. "And Laos probably hasn't gotten much new stuff lately. The Soviets have been busy fuckin' around in Africa, Afghanistan, South America and God knows where else. They've pretty well got Laos and Vietnam where they want 'em. I don't think Laos is real concerned Thailand is going to invade. Most of their tracking gear is probably to the north, aimed at the Chinese border. What are they worried about from the south? Fuckin' Cambodia? The goddamn Vietnamese own it."

"Laos ain't exactly got air traffic control problems, Jack," Tak Chao grinned. "I mean, you don't have anything like Tokyo International here. Not no reason to use a whole smear of radar equipment when there hardly anything around here that flies except for kites, man."

"Shut up," Hog growled.

"But I'm agreein' with you, Jack," the Thai merc stated.

"Shut up anyway," Wiley insisted. "You're givin' me a fuckin' headache with all that half-ass jive."

"I still think it's crazy," Viang Tha sighed, "but I'll agree to a recon of the airbase. We can decide whether to try to actually go through with your scheme after we've seen it and got a genuine idea about what we'd be up against."

"Fair enough," Hog said with a smile. "Let's get goin' before the birds figure we're statues and start shittin' on us . . ."

Hog fell silent when he heard voices and footsteps approaching their position. The strike force grabbed weapons. Wiley held up a hand to urge the others to hold their fire and stay calm. He gestured to Thani Son Chiang and Viang Tha to follow him. Both the Thai merc and the Laotian freedom fighter had silencers attached to the barrels of their CAR-15 rifles. The pair nodded. Hog pointed at the ground and clenched a fist, a signal for the others to stay put.

Wiley and his two Asian allies crept among the boulders toward the sound of the approaching group. They peered around the rocks and saw several Laotian soldiers. The troopers were chatting with each other, paying little attention to their surroundings. Obviously, they did not expect trouble. But they were still armed and potentially dangerous.

Hog would have been willing to let the soldiers stroll on by, but they were headed straight for the rock formations.

There were six troopers, enough to put up a fight. Gun-shots would be heard for miles in all directions. There were almost certainly more troops near by. Wiley decided they'd have to take the group out.

Viang Tha and Thani Son Chiang looked at the Ameri-can and nodded. They understood the rules of war. The soldiers had not caused them any harm, but they had to die anyway.

Wiley didn't have a silencer for his weapon. He leaned his CAR-15 against a boulder and drew a Puma combat knife from a belt sheath. Hog pointed at some boulders to the left. Viang Tha nodded. The Laotian moved to the po-sition. Wiley jerked a thumb toward another set of boulders to the right. Thani Son Chiang headed for this station.

The soldiers drew closer and walked between the rock formations. Thani Son Chiang crept through a gap between the boulders and slithered to a new position near the rear of the soldiers' little group. Hog and Viang Tha waited for the enemy to come to them. The troopers filed through a path in the rocks.

Hog Wiley grabbed the first man through the pass. He yanked the startled man forward and plunged the blade of his knife into the nape of his neck. Sharp steel severed the man's spinal cord and killed him instantly. Hog tossed the dead man aside, the knife still buried in the soldier's neck.

Viang Tha pointed his CAR at the astonished Laotian soldiers and squeezed the trigger. The silenced weapon rasped as six rounds hissed from the muzzle. Soldiers screamed. Bullets ripped into flesh. Two troopers were shot in the chest and face. They fell, knocking another man to the ground. The remaining soldiers shuffled backward and tried to unsling AK-47 rifles from their shoulders.

Thai Son Chiang was ready for them. The Thai merce-nary hit the pair with a burst of silenced 5.56mm rounds. Bullets split one trooper's spine. The other soldier tried to duck and lowered his head directly in the path of two CAR slugs.

Hog Wiley seized the hilt of his Puma and placed a boot

on the shoulder of the man he had killed. The Texan
yanked the blade from the neck of the corpse and returned
to the passage — it was filled with dead soldiers.

"Hold your fire!" he told Viang Tha and Thani Son
Chiang.

The Asians ceased fire and raised their weapons. Hog
climbed into the pathway and trampled the dead men,
checking for signs of life. He found the dazed sole survivor
among the corpses. Wiley killed the man quickly, driving
the point of his knife under the soldier's chin, through the
soft skin at the hollow of the jawbone until the blade
pierced the roof of his mouth and punctured the brain.
Confident all the soldiers were dead, Wiley emerged from
the passage and nodded to Viang Tha.

"Good work," he told the freedom fighter.

"It was easy," Viang Tha said with a shrug. "They barely knew what hit them. They certainly had no chance to
react."

"Feel kinda bad about this," Hog confessed. "Poor bastards just picked the wrong place to goof off. Still, we
didn't have any choice. Had to fuckin' do it. Just glad we
did it quick."

"They were careless," Thani Son Chiang stated as he
stepped from the pathway to join the others. "They were
not expecting trouble. We cannot expect all our opponents
will be this easy to defeat."

"You can sure as shit say that again," Wiley agreed.

"Why should I wish to repeat myself?" the confused
Thai asked.

"Never mind," Hog sighed. "Let's get the hell outta
here."

Chapter Eighteen

Stone awoke with a start. A stream of amber urine splashed across his nostrils and mouth, and a Laotian sentry laughed at Stone's disgust. The American coughed violently and vomited onto the ground.

"How are you feeling, Mister Stone?" Khong Noh's voice asked. "It appears your breakfast did not agree with you."

"I just don't . . . care much . . ." Stone rasped, trying to spit the sour taste of puke and urine from his mouth. "for your man's . . . choice of juice."

"Very good," Khong Noh laughed. "You've kept your sense of humor. I thought that stiff-upper-lip nonsense was suppose to apply to the British, not Americans."

Stone gazed up at the bandit chief. Khong Noh towered above him. Stone was lying spread-eagle on his back, wrists and ankles lashed to stakes driven into the ground. He was helpless, and Khong Noh's expression revealed cruel amusement. His eyes burned with hatred.

"What did you do . . . with the others?" Stone began, trying to catch his breath. "Loughlin? Hall and Franklin?"

"Maybe we chopped them up and cooked them for dinner," Khong Noh replied. "Maybe we'll make you eat their flesh. We could cook their testicles and stick them in your mouth. Or we could feed you your own instead. If we can find them after that kick I gave you."

"Yeah," Stone croaked. "You're a real hero, Khong Noh. You hit me twice when I couldn't hit back. You any good in a fair fight?"

"I've killed men with my bare hands, Stone," Khong Noh stated.

"So have I. Cut me loose and we could find out who's better."

"I don't have to prove anything, Stone," the bandit laughed. "I know I can take you. Frankly, that doesn't matter now. You and your friends are very stupid. I would have contacted the C.I.A., you know. Perhaps they would have paid more for you, and they certainly would have treated you better than the Communists will. But you and your friends abused my hospitality. We fed you, decent food, the same as our own. I discussed business with you as one gentleman to another. But you tried to escape, and you killed several of my men in the process."

"If you were in our position," Stone said. "Wouldn't you try to escape?"

"You killed Ban Xiang," Khong Noh declared, pointing an accusing finger. "He was my right-hand man and my best friend, Stone. How would you feel if a man killed your best friend? What would you do if you had him prisoner? If he lay staked out to the ground as you are?"

"I wouldn't turn anyone over to the Communists in Vietiane or Hanoi regardless of what grudge I had against him," Stone answered. "I might kill him, but I'd never do that."

"Too bad for you, Stone," Khong Noh hissed. "I'm not you."

"Will you tell me about the others, Khong Noh?" Stone asked. "Are they alive?"

"They're alive," the bandit chief answered. "The black man . . . What is that word for a negro? nigger? Isn't that what you call them?"

"I've never said that," Stone said.

"Then I think I will," the bandit smiled. "The nigger was struck by shrapnel. Lots of minor wounds and loss of blood, but nothing serious. My doctor stitched him up. You see, I bring my own doctor along whenever we go into the field. He's a very good doctor, but not good enough to help the men you killed. No one could help Ban Xiang after you gunned him down."

"He tried to shoot me in the back," Stone said gruffly. "What do you think I should have done? Tossed down my gun and started plucking flowers for the son of a bitch?"

Khong Noh suddenly stepped forward and slashed a foot between Stone's splayed legs. Stone screamed when the kick smashed into his sore genitals. The agony bolted through his body and twisted his stomach. Stone turned his head to the side and vomited again. There was nothing left in his stomach to throw up, so he dry heaved and spat out mucous and globs of blood.

"Come now, Stone," Khong Noh remarked. "I didn't kick you that hard. I wouldn't want to rupture you just yet. That might throw you into shock, which would be a blessing compared to what's going to happen to you before you reach Viangchan."

Stone turned his head away from the pool of vomit. The smell was disgusting and and the puke flowed down to his shoulder. He felt weak from the pain which burned at his crotch and the terrible wrenching his stomach muscles had suffered. Stone cursed himself for saying anything which might anger Khong Noh. He was not in a position to defy the bandit boss. Khong Noh could stomp him into jelly and there was nothing he could do about it.

If the bandit crippled him, any hope of escape would be lost. The chances of getting away seemed pretty bad, but there was still a chance. As long as Stone and his companions were still alive and able to move, there was a chance.

"You and your friends are going to pay for what you've done to my people, Stone," Khong Noh explained. "You remember what happened to Gorman? He caused many problems for me. Gorman hurt my reputation. I lost face because of him. Do you understand how important it is to us not to lose face?"

"I understand..." Stone replied, his voice barely a whisper. He nodded to make certain Khong Noh knew he was answering the question.

"Good," Khong Noh nodded. "Then you understand why Gorman had to be punished. Of course, he delivered you and the others to us. That reduced his punishment. He was simply executed. You saw that it was mercifully swift. You, however, have killed my people, including my best friend. That's a far more serious offense than Gorman was guilty of, and you have nothing to bargain with. Do you, Stone?"

"Information?" Stone offered, hoping he could bullshit the bandit chief and stall for time.

"Information?" Khong Noh laughed coldly. "Stone, you are going to tell us things you never realized you knew. We have to take care not to kill you, but as long as you can talk and, perhaps, use a finger and thumb to write with, we can inflict pain just about anywhere else as long as it won't be fatal."

He placed a foot on Stone's left knee and ground his heel into the joint. The American gritted his teeth. The pain was little more than discomfort, but Stone realized it would be easy for Khong Noh to dislocate or break his kneecap with a hard stomp or kick.

"You don't have to walk, for instance," the Laotian remarked. He removed his foot from Stone's knee and jammed a foot into Stone's left armpit. "And you won't need the use of this arm."

Khong Noh dug his toe into Stone's armpit. The nerve cluster located there transmitted sharp pain to Stone's agonized mind. The bandit shifted the sole of his boot against Stone's cheek, and smiled when he felt the American stiffen.

"We'd better not puncture your ear drums," Khong Noh remarked. "If you're deaf you won't be able to hear the government officials ask questions in the torture chambers at Vientiane. But, I don't think it will matter much if you can see. Maybe we'll just blind you in one eye to be sure."

Khong Noh moved the toe of his boot to Stone's left eye. The American closed his eye tightly. Terrible pressure against his eyelid jabbed the nerves of the eyeball. Stone gasped, but did not cry out. The pain was bad enough, but the terror was far worse. If Khong Noh pressed a little harder, Stone's eyeball would burst in its socket.

Instead, the bandit shoved with his foot and pushed Stone's face into the pool of vomit. The foul liquid filled Stone's nostrils as he tried to roll his face away from the mound of puke, but Khong Noh's foot kept his face stationary. Stone held his breath and hopelessly tried to slip his head free. At last, the bandit released him.

"Mustn't let you drown in your own vomit," Khong Noh chuckled. "Then you won't be around for everything we've got planned for you."

Stone turned his head away from the pool of vomit and spat out the puke. He vomited again. This time he was certain he was coughing his lungs out and dry heaving the lining of his stomach onto the ground. Khong Noh decided to leave him to ponder his fate and strolled to another section of the camp.

"Bloody coward bastard!" a familiar voice snarled. A loud groan followed.

Stone was relieved to hear Loughlin's voice. He had feared the Briton may have been killed by the explosion. Of course, Khong Noh had told him his friends were still alive, but he had only mentioned Dwayne Franklin. Nick Hall might have a fractured skull from the rifle butt to the head which had taken him out of the fight. Maybe Hall was already dead. If so, he might be the lucky one.

Stone could hear the sound of Loughlin's groans and curses. Khong Noh or some of his bandits were working on the Briton, probably giving him the same sort of treatment Stone had received. The ex-S.A.S. commando was tough. He would not break easily, but the bandits were not trying to break them yet. This was just the beginning.

Chapter Nineteen

The Laotian air base was surrounded by a barbed wire fence. There had been a report only two days ago about an attack on a border patrol eleven or twelve kilometers from the airbase, but the report had also stated that footprints left by the assailants indicated that they had fled east, toward the plateau region.

The Laotian soldiers at the base were not worried about this. No ragtag group of peasants would dare get within three kilometers of a compound guarded by guntowers and machineguns. The only aircraft present were helicoptors, left behind by the enemy when they pulled out of Laos and Vietnam.

"This place doesn't look so goddamn fuckin' tough to me," Hog Wiley whispered to Viang Tha as they peered through the elephant grass at the air base. "Can't be more than a hundred bastards stationed in that lil' old helipad."

"Less than that," the Laotian freedom fighter replied. "There's probably forty or fifty soldiers stationed there. But notice the observation towers? They've got Type 24 heavy machineguns mounted there."

"Type 24?" the Texan snorted. "Those old Chinese

chatterboxes must be older than the troops in the tower. Red China quit sendin' arms to Southeast Asia after the Russians muscled them outta Nam when Ho Chi Minh died."

"The Chinese were still in Laos after that," Viang Tha explained. "And don't underestimate those machine guns. The Type 24 fires a 7.92 round . . . not point-six-two, point *nine*-two. It's a water-cooled weapon, and the rate of fire is rather slow, compared to most automatic weapons, about four hundred rounds per minute. But the muzzle velocity is almost nine hundred meters per second."

"About three thousand feet per second?"

"That sounds right," the Laotian nodded. "The Type 24 uses an ammobelt. Two hundred and fifty rounds. The Type 24 can be used against aircraft or ground forces and it's very effective either way."

"I hope they give their choppers as much care as they seem to have for those fuckin' guns," Wiley remarked.

"They do," Viang Tha assured Hog. "Nice selection too. They have two UH-D gunships and a Boeing-Vertol Ch-47 Chinook."

"I recognize 'em," Hog stated. "The Chinook is the big sucker. Looks sorta like a giant hot dog with rotor blades at each end. You can haul more than forty men in one of those big bastards."

"Forty-four men," Viang Tha gave him the exact number. "The Chinook can carry more than five thousand kilos, but it doesn't move as fast as the Bell Uh-1D. The Bell is easier to maneuver, it can land in a smaller area and it has more than twice the range of the Chinook. She'll go more than five hundred kilometers without refueling."

"But you can only get about a dozen guys in a UH-1D," Hog frowned. "Well, fuck. We might just have to go with what we can get. Can you fly either one of these whirly-birds, Viang Tha?"

"Yes," the Laotian replied. "but I've had more experience with the Bell. I'd hate to take up a Chinook without a copilot."

"Hey, dude," Tak Chao grinned. "No need to cry in your beer. I can jockey that big momma like it's nobody's business. Outta sight, Jack."

"I think that means he can be your copilot," Thani Son Chiang explained. He seemed embarrassed by his fellow Thai merc's excessive use of slang.

"Now all we have to do is get inside the air base without getting cut down by machine guns," Viang Tha said dryly. "Seal a helicoptor and just fly away without being shot out of the sky."

"I don't think that will be as easy as you say," Lan Nhung frowned. The Laotian failed to recognize the sarcasm in his companion's voice. "After all, there are only eight of us."

"We go with what we've got," Hog said with a shrug. "Viang Tha? Thani Son Chiang? I want your best marksmen to pick off the guards in the gun towers. Kill the fuckers and they can't use those goddamn T-24 chatterguns. I want two men firin' at each tower to make sure the bastards are put outta action."

"Very well," Viang Tha agreed. "What about the rest of the soldiers?"

"We charge the fence, take out the sentries and blast the wire," Hog answered. "Now, you fellas see the building with the tall radio antenna? I want that motherfucker taken out double quick, as soon as we get through the fence."

"Is that your entire strategy, Hog?" Thani Son Chiang asked, astonished that the big man wanted to launch such a brutally simple attack against superior numbers.

"Ever hear how complicated things have a way of fuckin' up?" Hog said with a shrug. "Like they used to tell us in the army: 'Keep it simple, stupid.' Makes a lot of sense. 'Specially when you're in a goddamn hurry. So let's go!"

Two Laotian freedom fighters, including Lan Nhung, and two Thai mercenaries raised their rifles and opened fire. Bullets ripped into the guntowers. Enemy soldiers shrieked as slugs slammed into flesh. Hog led the charge as the rest of the strike force attacked the base.

The Laotian troops were amazed and startled to see a small group of guerrillas suddenly rise up from the elephant grass less than two hundred meters from the fence. A great hairy Caucasian hulk seemed to be the leader. The big man's CAR-15 looked like a toy in his massive fists, but flame jutted from the barrel and the bullets he fired were the real thing.

Three 5.56mm rounds sliced into the nearest sentry stationed by the wire. The guard screamed and fell, as other Laotian troops scrambled for weapons. A few were already armed and ready for action. They returned fire while their comrades rushed for the barracks, head shed and chopper hangars. Hog heard a voice cry out behind him. Enemy gunfire had struck down one his men.

"Goddamn," Hog growled. He dropped to the ground and yanked a grenade from his belt.

Several members of the attack force continued to fire at the enemy. The second guard at the fence went down with at least four rounds in his chest. Two other Laotian soldiers dropped their weapons and clawed at the bloodied bulletholes in their flesh. Hog yanked the pin from the grenade and hurled the blaster into the air base.

The grenade exploded, uprooting a fence post and dumping barbed wire to the ground. The strike force advanced, firing at the enemy soldiers and lobbing three more grenades at the base. The explosive eggs were aimed at the radio shack, which was actually the base headquarters. The first grenade blew the front of the flimsy building apart. The second and third grenades soared into the rumble and blasted the head shed to bits. Chunks of metal, wood, and human remains scattered in all directions.

The Laotian soldiers were disoriented and uncertain of what what to do next. Several followed their instincts and ducked behind cover to fire at Hog Wiley's little invasion force. An AK-47 round tugged at the Texan's shirtsleeve.

He barely noticed. Hog was too busy charging over the fallen wire to spray the enemy with 5.56mm slugs. Another soldier cried out and toppled forward, his face shot off by CAR lead.

Lan Nhung and the other snipers followed the first group of Hog's attack unit and supplied cover fire for the Texan, Tak Chao, Viang Tha and Thani Son Chiang. Grenades sailed into an enemy barracks. Two soldiers bolted outside to be struck down by a sheet of CAR fire. The grenades exploded and the barracks trembled before the roof caved in. Walls tumbled down, burying the soldiers under debris.

A pair of troopers opened fire with a Type 24 machine gun mounted at a chopper hangar. Big 7.92mm rounds sizzled past Hog Wiley as he dove to the ground. Viang Tha and Tak Chao also hit the dirt in time, but two other members of the unit were not as fortunate. Bullets chopped the Thai mercs into oblivion and hurled their bodies six feet backward.

Hog fired the last rounds from his CAR at the machine gun nest. He triggered the rifle against his hip and fired with one hand as he clawed another grenade from his belt. Hog dropped the empty CAR and pulled the pin from his grenade. The Texan noticed Thani Son Chiang had the same idea. Both men hurled grenades at the machine-gunners.

The explosive spheres rolled to the hangar. One soldier darted from the machine gun nest and kicked one grenade away from the hanger. It rolled under the carriage of a Bell UH-1D gunship. The guy tried to get rid of the second grenade, but the keen eye of Viang Tha had found the soldier. The Laotian freedom fighter fired his CAR and pumped three rounds into the trooper. The soldier went down and the grenades exploded.

The blast at the hangar ripped the Type 24 machine gun into mangled metal and tore the remaining trooper limb from limb. The other grenade erupted under the Bell chopper. The helicopter burst into a brilliant fireball. Shards of metal sliced air in all directions and flaming fuel spewed across the air base. Fire licked at the a column of metal drums located fifty meters from the gunships.

"That's the fuel supply!" Viang Tha shouted. "This whole place is gonna go up like dynamite factory!"

"Then let's get the fuck outta here!" Hog replied as he scooped up his CAR-15 and dashed toward the two remaining gunships.

The Texan's strike force headed for the nearest aircraft, the remaining Bell chopper. Viang Tha and Tak Chao shoved open the sliding doors and scrambled inside. Hog and Lan Nhung prepared to follow, but a stream of Kalashnikov rounds streaked from the belly of the Chinook. Lan Nhung convulsed wildly and fell against Wiley. The Texan dropped to the pavement. Lan Nhung's twitching body draped across Hog's back. Hot blood spurted from the dying man's veins, splashing Hog's eyes and face.

Thani Son Chiang fired his CAR at the Laotian troops stationed by the Chinook gunship. Bullets ricocheted against the metal underbelly, and the soldiers retreated. Hog Wiley shoved Lan Nhung's corpse aside and crawled into the Bell copter. Thani Son Chiang followed, still firing his weapon at the enemy trigger men. Another burst of Kalashnikov rounds raked the metal body of the Bell. Thani Son Chiang fell away from the threshold. His CAR skidded across the floor of the gunship. Blood bubbled from the Thai merc's left bicep.

Hog shoved the sliding doors shut and dropped on his belly as more AK-47 slugs pelted the Bell. Viang Tha and Tak Chao were in the cockpit, desperately trying to get the chopper off the ground.

"Hey, man!" Tak Chao's voice called to Wiley. "Sure be a bitch if we didn't have no juice in this flyin' chain-saw, wouldn't it?"

"Jesus motherfuckin' Christ!" Hog cursed. "Does this goddamn thing have fuel or not?"

"A full tank!" Viang Tha shouted to be heard above the roar of the rotor blades as the copter engine jumped to life.

"Tak Chao, you're a fuckin' asshole!" Hog snarled.

"Dig it, man," the Thai laughed. "I love you too, Jack!"

The Bell rose from the ground. The whine of bullets striking the undercarriage told them the enemy gunmen were still trying to take them out. Hog Wiley realized the danger was still enormous. A bullet to the fuel tank would have a fifty-fifty chance of igniting sparks which would set fire to the tank. In a confined space, the fuel would explode. And if a bullet damaged the cyclic controls or the rotor system, the Bell would come down fast and hard.

The fire at the air base continued to spread. Flames by the fuel supply heated the drums rapidly. The first one exploded and burning petrol shot across the base. A tide of flaming liquid splashed the Chinook gunship. The blaze then reached the enemy soldiers, scorching their lungs and rendering them unconscious. Their bodies began to cook in the raging fire.

Hog Wiley and the remaining members of his strike force felt the Bell gunship tremble as the shockwave of the explosion rocked the fleeing aircraft. Viang Tha and Tak Chao raised the Bell higher and raced from the flame-engulfed base below. More fuel drums exploded, and the impact sent shockwaves chasing after the Bell.

"Son of an Oklahoma whore," Hog muttered as the Bell shook violently. "How we doing?"

"We're alive, aren't we?" Viang Tha's voice replied.

Hog moved to Thani Son Chiang. The wounded mercenary had ripped open the sleeve surrounding his left arm. The bullet appeared to have punched clean through his bicep. The bone was probably broken, but at least the guy didn't have a chunk of metal stuck in him. Wiley examined the wound and opened a first aid kit on his belt.

"Hold on," Hog urged as he squeezed a tube of disinfectant over the wound. "This is gonna hurt a bit."

"It already hurts a bit," Thai Son Chiang answered through clenched teeth.

"You saved my ass back there," Hog commented, wrapping the arm with a field bandage. "I owe you, fella."

"Might consider a bonus for my final payment when we get back to Thailand," the mercenary suggested with a weak smile.

"A big bonus," Hog assured him.

"Well, Hog," Viang Tha called back to the Texan. "Your scheme worked. We've got a chopper. Of course, we also lost half our team in the process."

"I noticed," Wiley said gruffly. "Just fly the goddamn bird and I'll worry about handlin' my own guilt. Are we heading for the plateaus?"

"We will be," the Laotian replied. "As soon as we get this thing turned around."

"Man," Tak Chao commented with a nervous laugh. "This gig is turning into a real blast, Jack. Cat's pajamas, right-o daddy-o?"

"Keep it up, shithead," Hog growled. "And I'll shoot you myself."

Chapter Twenty

Sunset brought relief for Stone and Loughlin. Their naked upper torsos had been burned by the sun's rays. Their eyes were sore and blurry, their lips chapped and cracked from exposure.

"Have you had a nice rest, Stone?" Khong Noh inquired as he stood next to the helpless American prisoner.

"Ha...Have you..." Stone croaked hoarsely. "Got ...any...suntan lotion?"

"Very amusing, Stone," Khong Noh laughed. "We shall see if you still have a sense of humor in the face of agony and terror."

The bandits cut the bonds which held Stone's arms and legs to the stakes. They hauled him to his feet. His limbs burned as blood rushed into them. The lack of circulation left his arms and legs numb. The bandits dragged him to a tree and pulled his arms around the trunk to force him to embrace it. Handcuffs were snapped over his wrists, locking them together.

"I hope you're awake, Stone," Khong Noh commented at he stood next to the tree. "We're going to introduce you to a fine old custom used by the Chinese for centuries."

"Silk worms?" Stone groaned. The rough bark chaffed his sunburned chest. He tried to move his body back from the tree as far as his handcuffed arms would allow.

"Look here," Khong Noh said, as he held a thin bamboo rod near Stone's face. "We have a number of these. Just a skinny little reed. You wouldn't think there was anything sinister about it, now would you?"

Two bandits dragged Loughlin to another tree and forced his arms around the trunk. A second set of cuffs were used to lock his wrists together. The Briton turned his face toward Stone. His cheek was bruised by a dark welt and a patch of dried blood ran from his hairline to an eyebrow. One eye was swollen shut and his lips were covered with dried, scabbed skin. Stone wondered if he looked as bad as his friend. He sure felt like hell.

"Fancy . . . meetin' you . . . here, mate," Loughlin muttered in a weary, hoarse voice. He even managed a weak smile.

Something struck Stone's back. The blow stung, but it was not especially painful. Another blow followed, striking the same patch of skin. It hurt more the second time. The third stroke was worse. The fourth forced a gasp of pain from Stone's lips.

"You get the idea, Stone?" Khong Noh inquired. "You see, a proper bamboo flogging takes hours. At first the pain is mild. Then the muscles and skin begin to swell from the constant punishment. Your flesh becomes more tender and eventually it splits open . . . one layer of skin at a time. The raw, bleeding flesh is ever more sensitive to the flogging. But we won't let it go that far because it might kill you or put you in shock. This will be done very slowly and carefully, Stone. My people are experts when it comes to such things."

"You care enough to use the very best, huh?" Stone muttered.

"If that was a joke," Khong Noh mused. "I don't understand. It doesn't matter anyway. You won't feel like making many more jokes, Stone. You will beg for mercy and your pleas shall fall on deaf ears. We have many agonies planned for you and your fellow American scum."

"I'm British, remember?" Loughlin remarked. He flinched as a bamboo rod smacked his back.

"I found a pack of cigarettes in a pocket of the late Mr. Leo Gorman," Khong Noh remarked as a bandit continued to flog Stone with a bamboo reed. "I don't smoke much, but American cigarettes are really quite good."

The bandit leader took a cigarette from the pack and lit it with a Zippo lighter, also taken from Gorman's corpse. He blew smoke in Stone's face.

"This is interesting," Khong Noh remarked as he read the message on the cigarette pack. "Did you know the Surgeon General warns that cigarettes are dangerous?"

He tapped the ash from the end of his cigarette and blew on the glowing tip. The bandit smiled and jammed the burning tip into Stone's arm, sliding the cigarette into the crook of his elbow. Stone's face contorted with pain. Khong Noh removed the cigarette and smiled.

"Perhaps the Surgeon General had a point," he commented. He relit the cigarette and puffed it into life again.

Khong Noh then grabbed Stone's right hand and stabbed the burning end of the cigarette into the soft flesh between thumb and forefinger. Stone's arm trembled with pain. His fingers flexed as he tried to free himself of Khong Noh's grip. The bandit leader lit the cigarette again and jammed the glowing end into the base of Stone's thumb. The American cried out.

"These things really are nasty, aren't they?" Khong Noh mused. He thumbed the wheel of the Zippo and sparked the flame of the lighter. "This looks like it could be dangerous too . . ."

He shoved the lighter into Stone's right armpit. Flame ignited hairs and seared the sensitive flesh. The nerve cluster sent a terrible message shrieking through Stone's body. He convulsed against the tree. Bark scrapped his sunburned chest and the bamboo flogged his unprotected back again and again.

"Every inch of your body is going to be in agony," Khong Noh announced, as he ground the burning cigarette into Stone's skin at the last rib on his right side. "Not all at once and not enough to kill you, but we'll cause injuries which will last you for the rest of your life."

He moved to Stone's hands and held the lighter under his fingers. He flicked the lighter to life and held it to the American prisoner's fingers. Stone tried to wiggle his fingers away from the fire. He contorted and twisted as flesh burned. Khong Noh laughed.

"This is nothing, Stone," he warned. "Petty little wounds which you could take care of with some ice. No danger of infection or anything of that sort. You're really making more of a fuss about this than you should."

The bandit leader pinned Stone's left forearm to the tree trunk. He held the lighter at Stone's wrist. It burned flesh and heated the metal of the cuff. Stone clenched his teeth to stifle a cry of pain. Khong Noh stuck the flame into Stone's left armpit. The American slammed his forehead against the tree trunk as a spasm of pain jetted through his nervous system.

"Easy, Stone," Khong Noh urged. "Don't knock yourself unconscious. We can't have that. You'd miss all the exciting events we have planned for you."

Stone growled like a beast and lashed out a bare foot at Khong Noh. He realized the mistake as he made it. Being shackled with his arms around the tree made it impossible to deliver a fast, accurate kick. Khong Noh easily avoided Stone's foot and caught his ankle.

"That wasn't very smart, Stone," Khong Noh warned. He fired the Zippo again and held the flame to the little toe of the prisoner's foot.

Stone hopped on one foot, trying to pull his leg from Khong Noh's grasp, to free his foot from the terrible burning pain which consumed his toe. The bamboo whip caught him under the shoulder blade again and a wave of agony bolted up his spinal cord. Stone thought his brain would burst from the pain. He almost wished it would.

"You fuckin' cowards!" Nick Hall cried out.

A bandit chopped the edge of his hand across the bridge of Hall's nose, breaking it. Hall's protest ended abruptly, but the bandit backhanded him across the mouth, just to make certain he understood.

Khong Noh released Stone's foot and took another cigarette from the pack. He lit it and puffed gently as he watched the bandits steadily flog Stone and Loughlin. The Briton had received as many lashes as Stone, but Khong had not personally added cigarette burns and the flame of the Zippo lighter. The bandit leader was debating whether or not to give Loughlin a taste of this torture as well.

"Maybe later," he decided, tapping the ash from his cigarette.

Khong Noh grabbed Stone's hair and held his head as he pressed the burning tip of the cigarette into the side of the American's neck. Stone screamed. The bandits cheered approval for their leader's tactics. The men with the bamboo rods slashed harder with their instruments, eager to cause as much agony as their leader.

They all failed to notice the whirl of great blades cutting the air above until the helicopter was almost overhead. The bandits stared up at the aircraft with surprise. It was American-made, but many of the aircraft used by the Laotian military had been left behind by the Americans when they withdrew from Southeast Asia. Two bandits raised their weapons.

"Bau!" Khong Noh snapped a warning. "Put those guns down! Are you insane? You don't start shooting at government aircraft! Not unless you want to go to war with the entire Laotian armed forces!"

"What should we do, Khong Noh?" a bandit inquired.

"Lay down your weapons and hold up your hands so they don't feel threatened," the bandit leader instructed. "They're probably curious about what we're doing here. They might have simply passed by if you idiots hadn't raised your weapons."

Khong Noh sighed. "Well, Stone," he said in English.

"It looks as if the state found out about your little raid on the *Plateau des* P.O.W. camp quicker than we'd imagined. They've already sent helicoptors to search for you and your friends. That means we'll have to turn you over to the government already. Pity. We had so many more games to play together—but now you must become the property of the Laotian state."

The helicopter began to descend. The bandits laid down their arms and raised empty hands. Stone shuffled around the tree to watch the chopper. It was a Bell UH-1D, a real beauty, equipped with two .30 caliber machine guns and a fuselage big enough to carry fourteen men.

"If only you were on our side," Stone muttered wishfully.

The chopper lowered its nose slightly. Stone saw the pilots. Two Asians seated at the controls. There was something odd about them. The plexiglas distorted the view, but Stone thought they wore odd uniforms. Camouflage fatigues, he thought.

"Well, I'll be damned," he whispered.

"Well, mate," Loughlin sighed. He had moved into position to watch the gunship descend as well, but he could not see the cockpit from his position. "Looks like we've had it this time."

"Maybe not," Stone replied. "Maybe we just got a reprieve."

"What's that?" Loughlin asked.

"Get behind your tree for cover," Stone urged. "And pray that a miracle just dropped from the sky."

Chapter Twenty-one

The twin machine guns of the Bell UH-1D opened fire. Bullets raked the bandits, blasting half a dozen of Khong Noh's men before they knew what had happened. Others grabbed for weapons. A rope ladder swung from the Bell gunship and a big man with a shaggy head and beard climbed down the rungs. He held a CAR-15 in one ham-sized fist, firing it on full-auto as if it was a .22 target pistol.

"Bloody hell," Terrance Loughlin said with astonishment. "That's Hog! How'd he get here?"

"We'll ask him later," Stone replied, as he braced his feet against the tree and dug his fingers along the bark.

Pushing down with his legs and pulling with his arms, Stone slowly inched himself up the tree trunk. Luckily it was a young tree with few branches. None were very large and all were thin and flexible. Stone climbed higher.

Two of the bandits grabbed their weapons and turned toward the gunship. A wave of .30 caliber slugs chopped into their chests and pitched them to the ground. Others adopted a prone stance and fired at the Bell chopper. Bullets assaulted the metal undercarriage, ricocheting past Hog Wiley as he scrambled down the rope ladder.

Thani Son Chiang saw a bandit aim a Kalashnikov rifle at two men tied to a tree. The Thai merc lay on his belly within the chopper, the barrel of his CAR-15 protruding from the open doors. His wounded arm prevented him from climbing down the rope ladder, but he could still handle a gun.

The mercenary fired a three round blast. The bandit who was about to kill Hall and Franklin suddenly dropped his weapon. His head snapped to one side as the top of his skull vanished in a spray of crimson. Thani Son Chiang smiled with cold satisfaction and he searched for another target.

Hog Wiley spotted the muzzle flash of an enemy gunman's weapon. The bandit was firing from under the cover of a lump of ferns. Swinging his CAR toward the gunman, Hog sprayed the ferns with 5.56mm rounds. He saw a man's shape thrash about in the bush, then fall dead in the ferns.

Wiley glanced down at the ground. He reckoned it was about a ten foot drop. Hog let go of the ladder and plunged to the ground. He bent his knees on impact and rolled forward, head lowered and rifle held close to his chest. Hog rolled smoothly and landed on one knee, swiftly bringing the plastic stock to his shoulder.

Stone continued to climb the tree. Blood oozed from under his finger and toenails. A branch bent against his arm. He pulled himself higher and scaled the tree until the branch slid from under his arm. The tree was thinnest at the top. Stone gripped the narrow trunk with his fists and pulled himself hand over hand, as if climbing a rope. His knees hugged the trunk.

The tree began to sway. Stone climbed higher. The top of the tree bowed from his weight. He ducked his head and pulled himself higher. Suddenly, Stone began to slide backward. The tree bent toward the ground. Branches snapped against the steel links of the handcuffs. Stone's legs dangled as he rode the tree backward. He moved faster. Branches slid under his torso. The limbs were flexible and gave way under his weight. The top leaves of the tree touched the ground as the trunk arched into a great bow.

Stone felt the ground beneath his bare feet. The last springy branches slipped between his arms and the tree bounced back to an erect posture. Stone sighed with relief. His wrists were still cuffed together, but he was free at last. Loughlin looked at his friend with envy. The tree Loughlin was bound to had a great fork at the trunk just above his head. The thick branches prevented him from using the same tactic Stone had employed.

"Hang on," Stone urged.

"I'll keep," the ex-S.A.S. trooper replied. "Get that bastard Khong Noh before the bleedin' snake gets away."

"You bet," Stone assured him.

Suddenly, a burst of 9mm rounds slashed at Stone and Loughlin's position. A bandit had decided not to allow their prisoners to be taken by the rescue team. Stone threw himself to the ground. Loughlin could only duck his head and hug the tree. bullets punched the trunk between the Briton's arms. Chips of bark spat from the tree. Remarkably, a parabellum struck the chain of his handcuffs. The steel link popped.

Loughlin's arms swung free. He fell backward and landed on his backside, amazed by the freak accident which had freed him. Hog Wiley trained his CAR on the bandit who had tried to kill his friends. The Laotian held a French MAT-49 submachine gun. He rushed toward Stone and Loughlin's position, determined to finish them off.

"No way, cocksucker," Hog growled as he nailed the bandit with three 5.56mm rounds between the shoulder blades.

The man's arms flew apart, throwing the MAT subgun toward the trees. He fell on his face, twitched twice and died once. Loughlin scrambled from cover and scooped up the dead man's subgun. He glanced at Hog. The Texan gave him a thumbs up and smiled at the Briton. Loughlin nodded and hurried to Stone's side.

"Hold your arms out and I'll liberate you," the Briton invited.

"Don't squeeze the trigger until I'm ready," Stone urged. "And make sure that thing is on semi-auto first. I just want the cuffs off. Like to keep all of my fingers."

"Does this weapon fire semi-auto?" Loughlin wondered.

"Shit," Stone rasped. "Take the magazine out. There should be one round in the chamber."

The Briton obeyed. Stone extended his arms and pulled his wrists apart as far as the short chain of the handcuffs allowed. Loughlin pressed the muzzle of the MAT against the center of the chain.

"Ready?" he asked.

"Do it," Stone replied.

The Briton squeezed the trigger. A single 9mm round shrieked from the barrel. It punched through the steel links. The chain snapped in two. Stone flexed his fingers and stretched his arms. Bruised, bloodied and burned, the ex-Green Beret was still ready to fight.

Most of Khong Noh's bandits were already dead, seriously wounded, or dying. The Bell climbed into the sky and sprayed the surrounding area with .30 caliber slugs, blasting the bamboo and brush where the bandits had run when the shooting began. Hog Wiley rushed to the tree where Nick Hall and Dwayne Franklin were still held captive. He drew his Puma and quickly sliced through the ropes.

"Behind you!" Franklin shouted.

Hog whirled and raised his knife. He glimpsed a shape with an AK-47 in its fists. Wiley's arms swung hard, hurling the Puma. Six inches of sharp steel struck the gunman in the throat. The knife sunk to the hilt, until the point jutted from the back of the bandit's neck. The man dropped his Kalashnikov and crumbled to the ground.

"Jesus," Franklin rasped. "I ain't never seen nobody throw a knife like that before!"

"Me neither," Hog admitted. "Reckon all those years of mumblety peg playin' was worth something after all."

A pair of bandits bolted from the jungle, driven out by the hailstorm of machine gun bullets fired from the gunship. Loughlin blasted the pair with a salvo from the MAT-49 submachine gun. Two parabellums ripped into one man's chest and sent his dying body to the ground. Another bullet caught the second bandit in the shoulder. He reeled from the impact, a Type-56 assault rifle falling from his hands.

"Hell," Loughlin cursed when the MAT clicked. "Bloody thing is empty."

The wounded bandit drew a knife from his belt and lunged at the Briton. Loughlin raised the empty subgun. The blade struck the barrel of Loughlin's weapon. The ex-S.A.S. man slammed the frame of the MAT-49 into the bandit's wrist, striking the knife from his grasp. Loughlin rammed the stock of the empty weapon into his opponent's solar plexus. The man doubled over with a groan.

Loughlin slashed the side of his hand to the nape of the bandit's neck. The Laotian hood fell to all fours. Loughlin raised his arm, bent the elbow and brought it down on the base of his opponent's neck. Vertebrae crunched. The man fell to the ground, his neck broken.

Stone had grabbed the nearest weapon to assist his British friend. His hand closed around a rock the size of a baseball. However, Loughlin had handled the situation well enough, but Stone noticed another threat. The barrel of a large pistol emerged from a section of elephant grass. Stone recognized the weapon. It was a Soviet Stechkin machinepistol, aimed at Loughlin.

He hurled the rock. It struck the Stechkin and sent it flying from numb fingers. Stone remembered which bandit carried a Russian machinepistol. It was Khong Noh. And

Stone was more than eager to get his hands on the filthy bastard.

The bandit leader rose up from the grass, his hands poised like twin talons. Stone didn't expect Khong Noh to confront him without trying to flee first, and he almost ran right into him. Khong Noh lashed a roundhouse kick to the American's ribs. Stone groaned and staggered. Khong Noh hooked the heel of his palm to the side of Stone's head.

The blow knocked Stone to the ground. He rolled onto a shoulder and landed on one knee. Khong Noh raised a hand to deliver a swordhand chop. The ex-Green Beret jumped up from the ground and drove both fists into his opponent's torso. The double punch knocked Khong Noh backward. Stone swung a high Tae Kwon Do kick at the bandit's face. Khong Noh's head flashed out of the path of the flashing foot.

Stone's balance was thrown off when his foot failed to connect. He pivoted awkwardly on one foot. Khong Noh hooked a kick to Stone's back, hitting him full force above the left kidney. The kick sent Stone plunging headlong into a number of bamboo stalks. Khong Noh slashed the side of his hand at the nape of Stone's neck.

Stone turned and blocked the attack with a forearm. He jabbed a fist to Khong Noh's breastbone and followed with a left hook to the bandit's jaw. Stone hit his opponent on the point of the chin with a karate punch. Khong Noh stumbled backward. Stone snap-kicked the bandit in the midsection, the ball of his foot striking Khong Noh hard in the stomach.

Khong Noh folded from the kick, but then managed to thrust both hands under Stone's ribs, rigid fingers stabbing like knives. Stone gasped, his breath driven from his lungs by the vicious double spearhand stroke. Khong Noh butted his forehead into Stone's breastbone.

The American staggered. Khong Noh's hand streaked toward Stone's face, two arched fingers aimed at the eyes. Stone jerked his head aside. The Laotian stumbled forward and Stone hit him under the jaw with the heel of his right palm.

Khong Noh fell backward. Stone grabbed his opponent's right wrist and twisted his arm, locking it at the elbow. Stone's foot hooked Khong Noh in the lower abdomen. The bandit groaned and doubled up. Stone prepared to deliver another kick, but Khong Noh suddenly dropped to the ground. He caught himself on his left palm and a knee as he lashed a sweeping kick at Stone's ankles.

The bandit's leg chopped Stone's feet out from under him. Stone landed on his back, still holding onto his opponent's arm. Khong Noh rolled with Stone's movement and lashed a kick into Stone's gut. His left hand clawed at Stone's face. The American vet clubbed the attacking fingers aside with his right forearm and punched the Asian in the mouth.

Khong Noh fell back, but managed to swing another kick at Stone. The American released Khong Noh's arm and pumped both fists into his opponent's shin, to block the kick. The bandit chief quickly rolled away and rose to his feet. Stone got up just as fast, and the pair squared off once more.

Stone feinted with his left hand and stomped a sidekick for Khong Noh's kneecap. The bandit moved his leg to avoid the kick, and slashed a clawed hand at Stone's right arm. Khong Noh's other hand stabbed a hard spearhand thrust to Stone's sternum. The blow stunned the American. He staggered away from Khong Noh. The bandit's right leg swooped into a crescent kick, smashing his opponent in the side of the face.

Stone fell to the ground. His head felt as if his skull had been split open. His chest was constricted, lungs refusing to draw air. Khong Noh staggered toward his fallen opponent. He was breathing heavily. Blood poured from his crushed mouth. He uttered ugly animal sounds, because the hinges of his jawbone had been dislocated by blows received during the battle. Stone was good. Very good. But

Khong Noh had won. He raised his boot and prepared to stomp the American's face into pulp.

Stone jerked his head aside. The heel of Khong Noh's foot hit ground near Stone's right ear. He thrust his left fist upward and drove a devastating punch between Khong Noh's legs with all the force he could muster. Knuckles smashed into the bandit's genitals. A testicle burst. Khong Noh howled in horrible agony, and doubled over.

Stone's right hand shot upward, fingers stiff in a spear-hand thrust. The tips of his fingers struck Khong Noh in the center of the throat. The bandit's windpipe collapsed. Khong Noh fell backward. His hands clawed at his crushed throat as he twitched wildly on the ground. The bandit kicked and thrashed in hopeless fury. Then his body sprawled in final defeat, and the last flicker of life vanished.

Mark Stone propped himself up on an elbow and watched Khong Noh die. His vision was blurred, and he felt as if he might pass out at any moment, but he was able to breath again. Dragging himself to a kneeling position, he slowly attempted to rise but fell back to all fours. His head was spinning. He nearly blacked out.

"There you are," a voice boomed. "I've been lookin' all over the fuckin' place for you."

Hog Wiley marched forward and scooped up Stone with one brawny arm. He braced Stone under the arms and dragged him toward the clearing. The Bell gunship had landed. Loughlin was poised by the chopper, a Kalashnikov rifle in his fists. Hall and Dwayne were already inside the helicopter. Hog dragged his buddy to the whirlybird. Loughlin clucked his tongue and grabbed Stone's legs.

"Damn, Hog," the Briton complained. "What if he has internal injuries or a damaged spine?"

"Then he'd surely be shit outta luck anyway, wouldn't he?" the Texan replied, with his own brand of country wisdom.

"I thought you were supposed to be resting up back in

the States, Hog," Stone said weakly.

"I'm all healed up," Wiley grinned. "Ain't you noticed?"

They hauled Stone into the gunship. Hog and Loughlin joined the others inside. The Texan shoved the sliding doors shut and the Bell chopper rose into the twilight sky. Stone smiled as he stared up at Hog's face.

"Where'd you get the chopper?" he asked. "Stole it from the Laotians?"

"Damn right," Wiley replied. "We figure we can just fly down south aways, toward the Cambodian border. Nobody's gonna figure we're anything special 'til we cut across the border into Thailand. Might have us a long walk to Bangkok, but what the hell, we can use the exercise."

"We'll be lucky if they don't shoot us down," Loughlin said sourly. "This is one damn crazy plan, Hog."

"Glad you approve," the Texan laughed. "Don't fret, buddy. Crazy has worked just fine so far, ain't it?"

"Yeah," Stone smiled. "Thanks for getting us outta there, Hog. I owe you, buddy."

"Hell," Wiley shrugged. "You would'a done the same for me. Might not've done quite as good a job, but you would've done the same."

"I just hope we don't run into any more trouble," Stone commented. "I think I've had enough for one day."

The steady drone of the chopper blades was slowly lulling him to sleep.

"Don't worry, buddy boy," Hog crooned. "Just leave the driving to me. We'll be home in no time."

It was the last thing Stone heard before he drifted away into dreams of sunshine and freedom.

Watch for

STONE: M.I.A. HUNTER

the next exciting novel in
the explosive series from Jove

coming in February!

**Finding them there
takes a new breed of courage.
Getting them out takes a new kind of war.**

M.I.A. HUNTER

by Jack Buchanan

Trapped in a jungle half a world away,
they're men no one remembers — no one but former
Green Beret Mark Stone and the daring men who
join him. They're taking on an old enemy with
a new kind of war. And nothing is going to stop them
from settling their old scores.

___ M.I.A. HUNTER	0-515-08824-2/$2.95	
___ M.I.A. HUNTER: CAMBODIAN HELLHOLE	0-515-08771-8/$2.75	
___ M.I.A. HUNTER: HANOI DEATHGRIP	0-515-08806-4/$2.75	
___ M.I.A. HUNTER: MOUNTAIN MASSACRE	0-515-08770-X/$2.75	
___ M.I.A. HUNTER: EXODUS FROM HELL	0-515-08544-8/$2.75	
___ M.I.A. HUNTER: BLOOD STORM	0-515-08823-4/$2.75	

Available at your local bookstore or return this form to:

JOVE
THE BERKLEY PUBLISHING GROUP, Dept. B
390 Murray Hill Parkway, East Rutherford, NJ 07073

Please send me the titles checked above. I enclose _____. Include $1.00 for postage
and handling if one book is ordered; add 25¢ per book for two or more not to exceed
$1.75. CA, IL, NJ, NY, PA, and TN residents please add sales tax. Prices subject to change
without notice and may be higher in Canada. Do not send cash.

NAME _____

ADDRESS _____

CITY _____ STATE/ZIP _____

(Allow six weeks for delivery.)   **MIA**

*It begins beyond anything
you have ever experienced before...*

TNT

by Doug Masters

Endowed with superhuman abilities
by the fallout of an atomic blast,
Tony Nicholas Twin has become
as deadly a killer as he is skilled a lover.
Sophisticated and outrageous,
exotic and erotic,
he'll take on any challenge.
He has to—he's TNT.

____ *TNT*	0-441-81310-0—$2.75
____ *TNT: THE BEAST*	0-441-05153-7—$2.75
____ *TNT: SPIRAL OF DEATH*	0-441-81311-9—$2.75
____ *TNT: THE DEVIL'S CLAW*	0-441-14297-4—$2.75
____ *TNT: KILLER ANGEL*	0-441-44203-X—$2.75
____ *TNT: RITUAL OF BLOOD*	0-441-81312-7—$2.75

Available at your local bookstore or return this form to:

CHARTER
THE BERKLEY PUBLISHING GROUP, Dept. B
390 Murray Hill Parkway, East Rutherford, NJ 07073

Please send me the titles checked above. I enclose _____. Include $1.00 for postage
and handling if one book is ordered; add 25¢ per book for two or more not to exceed
$1.75. CA, IL, NJ, NY, PA, and TN residents please add sales tax. Prices subject to change
without notice and may be higher in Canada. Do not send cash.

NAME _____

ADDRESS _____

CITY _____ STATE/ZIP _____

(Allow six weeks for delivery.)   C6A